D1518972

FIANCÉ BY FATE

AN ANYONE BUT YOU NOVEL

JENNIFER SHIRK

Entangled Publishing, LLC
2614 South Timberline Road
Suite 109
Fort Collins, CO 80525
Visit our website at www.entangledpublishing.com.

Bliss is an imprint of Entangled Publishing, LLC. For more information on our titles, visit http://www.entangledpublishing.com/category/bliss

Edited by Stacy Abrams and Alycia Tornetta
Cover design by Jessica Cantor

ISBN 978-1-50286-883-1

Manufactured in the United States of America

First Edition April 2014

Bliss
an Entangled imprint

This book is for you, Mom, because I know you've been to more than a few psychic readings in your lifetime.

Chapter One

You're not doing anything wrong.

Sabrina Cassidy took a deep breath and waited for the psychic to shuffle the cards.

You're not doing anything wrong.

She repeated the thought again for good measure—and because she liked to hear herself think.

Eating an entire cake? Sure, she could feel guilty. Lying on a résumé? Oh yeah, she'd certainly feel terrible about that one. But asking a psychic for information on her fiancé? Not a chance. She was sure any woman in her position would do exactly the same thing.

Pretty sure, anyway…

The psychic placed the third Fate tarot card down on the table with such careful attention to spacing that Sabrina was almost afraid to breathe on it. The woman seemed a stickler for details—except when it came down to her name: Madame Butterfly. The psychic was neither Japanese nor even

Fiancé By Fate

really *female* for that matter, but so far she seemed to know what she was talking about, so Sabrina was willing to let those things slide.

Sabrina glanced at her friend, sitting next to her. Maddie's eyes were looking sleepy, and she was trying hard to stifle a yawn. Sabrina had to admit, watching Madame Butterfly was a little like watching a slug race. They had already been there for more than twenty minutes and were just starting to get to the good stuff.

It was Maddie's suggestion that they come to get their fortunes told tonight. She thought Sabrina needed some fun, a distraction to help her forget about her recent fiancé problems. But Sabrina took the readings much more seriously than that. From the moment she and David had met, she had known it wasn't merely by chance. It was something more — the date, the timing. David was her destiny. And although she and her fiancé were on a temporary break right now, Sabrina knew in her heart they would be together again.

Of course, if she could hear that same thing from the psychic, it'd make her feel much better.

"I see a man in your future…" the psychic began in a raspy voice. His — *her* — Adam's apple bobbed up and down as she closed her eyes and laid her palms on the cards. Sabrina blinked and tried hard to focus on what she was saying and not on the hair of Madame's knuckles.

"A man. Wow, that narrows it down," Maddie muttered. Sabrina shushed her.

Madame Butterfly opened one false-lashed eye and aimed a definitive glare at Maddie, then continued on. "He's very handsome."

Sabrina shot a knowing grin at Maddie. David *was*

handsome. And smart. And successful. He was just finishing his orthopedic surgery residency at Mass General.

The psychic opened her eyes, tapping a long, painted-blue nail on top of one of the cards. "He's wearing a white coat."

Sabrina gasped. "David's a doctor. That could be his lab coat you're talking about."

Madame Butterfly nodded emphatically. "Yes, I see that."

"*Now* you see that," Maddie added, folding her arms over her chest.

It was Sabrina's turn to glare at her friend. "Maddie, please. Don't make me kick you out of here."

"You can't kick me out. I'm the one who paid."

The table suddenly buzzed. Madame leaned forward and blew out her candle. "I'm afraid our time is up," she said in a regretful tone. "Please exit to your left."

"What? But wait," Sabrina pleaded. "One last thing. I have to know…do you see us…?" She tried to calm her voice. "I mean, will David and I get back together in my future?"

Madame Butterfly studied the cards for several agonizing seconds, then looked straight into Sabrina's eyes. "Yes. Most definitely."

I knew it! Sabrina elbowed Maddie with a grin. "I told you we were meant to be."

"Ah," the psychic said, waving a finger in Sabrina's face, "you must be careful with this knowledge. You are still the creator of your own destiny." A dry smile slowly kicked at the corners of her mouth. "Don't overlook the journey, my dear."

Sabrina frowned. *Journey?* "But I don't understand. You said David and I would get back together."

Madame Butterfly stood and threw her heavily ringed hands in the air. "Sorry. You want more information, you need to pay. And also reschedule. I have an appointment waiting."

Maddie grabbed Sabrina's arm and yanked her up. "We're *not* paying more. But thanks for the entertainment. It was a real hoot."

Sabrina allowed herself to be pulled out the door, even though she was seriously tempted to shill out the extra money. A little "journey" clarification would be nice to have.

Once they were outside, Sabrina turned to her friend. "Hey, just so you know, that wasn't entertainment. That was for real. Everything Madame Butterfly said was spot-on."

Maddie snorted. "Easy for you to say. At least you got 'white coat.' All I got was 'lots of hair' in my relationship destiny. Now I'm going to have to make a guy remove his shirt before I date him."

Sabrina laughed. "Aha! I knew you believed."

"I *don't*." Her friend bit her lip, then grinned. "Well, maybe a little," she admitted. "Now I need a drink. Let's stop over there." She pointed across the street to a Tex-Mex bar and restaurant. "You owe me a margarita after that one."

"Okay. Deal."

The truth was, all that psychic-journey stuff gave Sabrina a headache and she needed a drink, too. Plus, it was unusually warm for an October night in Boston.

Tons of people were out walking along the streets in the Back Bay, and although the restaurant was packed, they managed to snag a high-top table in the corner of the bar.

After the waitress took their drink orders, Maddie scanned the crowd and grinned. "I think we struck gold. Lots of hotties here tonight," she said, waggling her eyebrows up and down.

Sabrina shook her head but glanced around anyway. Yeah, there were some cute guys. But she only had eyes for one. And unfortunately, he wasn't there. "You can meet your hottie. I'm an engaged woman, remember?"

Maddie pursed her lips. "You *were* an engaged woman."

"David said this split was just temporary while he figured some things out. Besides, you heard what Madame Butterfly said. We *will* be getting back together. As far as I'm concerned, I'm still engaged."

Maddie blew her wavy blond hair out of her eyes. "Now I'm sorry I suggested going to that psychic. I was hoping it would get you to forget about David and his 'I think we need a little separation' theory."

Sabrina lifted her chin. "Hey, it happens to be a good theory."

"Says David."

"No, says *me*, too. It's actually very mature when you think about it. Maybe we did rush into our engagement a little. Better to take a small step back now and make sure this is what he really wants. It's a big commitment, and I appreciate that he's not taking it lightly." Although a little niggle of doubt—despite what Madame Butterfly had said—wormed its way into her thoughts. She pasted on a bright smile when the waitress brought their drinks and wiped the thought out of her mind.

After the waitress turned away, Maddie lifted up her glass in a toast. "Well, here's to a hottie for me and good karma for you and David."

Sabrina smiled. "I'll drink to that." She took a healthy sip and swallowed appreciatively. The margarita was the perfect combination of sweet and sour and as she licked the salt from her lips, she enjoyed the heady kick of the tequila. She was such a lightweight when it came to alcohol.

Maddie leaned in with a wicked grin. "Remember when you talked me out of that tattoo for my birthday? Well, I was thinking…" A strange look crossed her face and she trailed off.

"You were thinking what?"

"Nothing." Maddie's eyes grew round, and then she ducked her head. With a shaky hand, she lifted her margarita to her lips and downed half of it. "I was thinking nothing. Let's finish our drinks and get out of here."

"But we just got here, and you said there were lots of hotties."

"Not that many," Maddie said, her voice escalating. "In fact, did I mention I needed glasses? Hey, I have a great idea! Let's go get my eyes examined. I think there's a Four Eyes around the corner."

"What's the matter with you?" She glanced behind her to see what had Maddie in such a tizzy, and when she did, she immediately understood.

Her fiancé, David, was standing on the other side of the bar, talking to a beautiful redhead. Sabrina's heart dropped further when he grinned at something the woman said, then handed her a glass of wine.

Sabrina bit her lip until it throbbed. David. With another woman. She had to look away, or she was going to be sick.

Maddie placed her hand over Sabrina's and squeezed.

"Hey, I'm sorry you had to see that, but pull it together. Don't sit here and let him do this to you. You should go confront him."

Her chest hurt, and she wanted to scream, but she shook her head instead. "No. I couldn't do that," she said, trying to control the tremor in her voice. "David wouldn't want a scene."

Maddie scowled. "David wouldn't want a scene? Forget what that jackass wants."

"No, I—I can't."

"Well, don't you worry," her friend said, patting her hand. "I personally love a good scene, so I'll be more than happy to cause one for you."

Maddie sliding off her stool pulled Sabrina from her daze. She grabbed Maddie's arm. "No. Don't. It's nothing. I've seen her before. I think she's a doctor at the hospital."

Maddie looked back at David with her eyes narrowed. "A coworker? Maybe. He's not touching her or making any googly eyes, I'll give him that much. There are two other men with them, too."

Relief flooded her senses, and she was able to breathe again. "See?" She picked up her drink and took a healthy gulp. "It's business. Now sit down before he sees us. *Please.*"

"Oh, fine," her friend huffed. "Looks like they're going into the restaurant now anyway." She sat back down but still looked petulant. "Honestly, Sabrina, you should go over there and say hello. If he's truly out on business, then neither of you have anything to feel guilty about."

That was true. But a nauseating sinking of despair held her immobile. What if it *was* a date? What would she do? She couldn't let him go so easily. She finally thought she could have a family and home of her very own. After everything she'd been through, was that too much to want for herself?

Maddie tilted her head. "Your silence is incriminating. You know what I would do if I were you?"

She was afraid to know, but still asked, "What?"

"Retaliate."

"Retaliate," she repeated. She cocked an eyebrow. "What are we, fifteen?"

Maddie shrugged a shoulder, then opened her purse and pulled out a copy of *Boston* magazine. "Okay, maybe 'retaliate' is the wrong word. But dating while he makes up his mind is a good strategy. Imagine if David saw you with one of these guys. That so-called temporary break of his would be on permanent hiatus."

Sabrina peered down at the article entitled "New England's Most Eligible Bachelors" and rolled her eyes. "Oh my gosh. Are you serious?"

"As a heart attack."

"Well, put it away before you give me one. I'm not interested in dating any eligible bachelors to make David jealous."

"Why not? If David is playing the field, you should, too."

"He's *not* playing the field." Maddie just didn't get it. Sabrina didn't want to play games. At almost thirty years old, she didn't have the time or patience for them. She and David had been together for three years and it had been wonderful—a lovely taste of what it was like to be loved and accepted into a family. "Look, I appreciate what you're trying to do, but I don't want to date anyone else."

Maddie ignored her last comment by burying her nose in the article. "Check out this guy. He's even from Boston."

Sabrina grudgingly looked. And wish she hadn't. Jack Brenner's all-too-handsome face stared back at her. He was posed with his arms crossed, wearing a designer tuxedo, tieless with his shirt undone at least four buttons down from the collar. His thick, dark hair looked playfully mussed, as if some woman had just run her fingers through it.

Sabrina swallowed hard. Good Lord, for a man who worked in finance, he sure had Hollywood-chiseled looks. Unfortunately, he also had that same cocky grin he wore the last time she'd spoken to him—and that was enough to ground her back down to reality.

She shoved the magazine away. "Definitely not that one."

Maddie did a double take at his picture, then frowned. "Are you kidding me? Why? He's the best-looking one in the bunch."

"Well, I can speak from personal experience that he's all too aware of that, too."

Maddie's mouth hung open. "You've met Eligible Bachelor Number Three and you didn't introduce him to your bestest single girlfriend?"

"Trust me. If I had, we wouldn't be friends anymore. He's my boss's son and one of the mutual-fund wholesalers at my company. Thankfully, he covers the state of Connecticut, so he's rarely in the Boston office. Small favors, since he's a complete and total player."

Her friend winced. "A dog, huh?"

"I'm afraid so."

Maddie looked back at his picture longingly. "Yeah, I guess the article does mention he's gone through quite a string of women. But I don't know. Dogs can be fun.

Sometimes all they need is the right trainer."

Sabrina just shook her head. Becoming another notch on someone like Jack Brenner's bedpost held no appeal to her. The last thing she wanted was to be bounced around in her love life like she'd been bounced around foster homes as a kid. That kind of hollowness was not something she' d easily forget, which was why she craved stability. And David gave her that. Besides being handsome and intelligent, he was grounded and levelheaded. David's parents loved her, too. Even if she took out Madame Butterfly, there were still so many signs…

"Is he as handsome as his picture?" Maddie asked with a sigh.

Sabrina wrinkled her nose at her friend's fawning. It never failed. Whenever Jack Brenner entered a room, women felt compelled to fling their panties in his direction like he was some modern-day Elvis He had that kind of effect on women.

On all women except her, that is.

Sabrina shrugged. "I guess so."

A minor lie. Jack Brenner was a *thousand* times better-looking in person. Even though she was engaged, she could admit that much to herself. After all, any woman would have to be dead and buried in the grave a month not to notice. But that didn't change the fact that he was heartless and self-centered. He didn't even have the decency to come back to town when his father was in the hospital last month. The fact that he could so easily dismiss his family in a time of crisis was yet another reason why she couldn't stand the man.

Maddie stuffed the magazine back in her purse. "I have to hand it to you. You must be head over heels in love to ignore someone like that."

"I definitely am. David is worth the wait."

"Well, if I were you and anything happens with your engagement to David—or maybe I should say *doesn't* happen with him—I'd zero in on this guy in a heartbeat the next time I saw him."

Sabrina laughed. Yeah. Right. Get mixed up with a playboy like Jack who ate up women who threw themselves at him like they were chocolate bonbons? No. Thank. You. There was no chance of that happening, even if she and David never got back together. Which was highly unlikely in itself.

But she knocked on the wood table for luck anyway.

Maddie eyed her. "All I'm saying is keep an open mind. Don't get your hopes up that David will be ready to commit just because of a few superstitions and the premonition of a cross-dressing psychic."

"I *am* keeping an open mind. I may not be Madame Butterfly, but I can safely predict that Jack Brenner is one man who will never, ever be a part of my future."

• • •

Jack Brenner walked across his father's penthouse and stared out the window into the night. The Boston skyline was illuminated before him and he felt content being back in the city he'd grown up in. This was where he belonged. It took some time, but he'd paid his dues and was ready to make the next step in eventually taking over control of Brenner Capital Investments. He assumed that was why his father had transferred him back to Boston, to make the transition easier. Jack couldn't wait to get started. He loved his job, and he did it well. Aside from his family, this company was the one thing he could say he was truly passionate about.

It was a part of him.

The front door suddenly opened, and his father walked in. Leonard Brenner smiled and extended his arms wide as soon as his gaze landed on Jack. "I'm glad you finally made it, son. You look great."

"Thanks. It's been a while," he said, giving his father an extra clap on the back. He stepped away and tried not to appear obvious as he assessed his father's appearance. At least on the surface, his dad looked fit and healthy.

Taking a deep breath, Jack hesitated, not sure he wanted to hear the answer to his next question. "So…how do you feel?"

His dad gave him a crooked smile as he rubbed his chest. "The old heart's still ticking, if that's what you want to know. I'm sorry to tell you that it'll take more than a little angina to force me to retire." His smile grew wider, and he looked at Jack with a thoughtful expression. "You know, I'm really glad you're back. Maybe it was worth getting sick to have you home where you belong."

Jack tried to smile, too, but a part of him was still worried about his father. He wished he could have been at the hospital when his father was admitted last month. He would have liked to talk with the doctors personally. Since his mom's death, his dad was everything to him. Unfortunately, his former girlfriend didn't quite have the same attitude when it came to family matters and neglected to pass on the message until he'd already been discharged from the hospital.

"Yeah, I'm glad to be back. The traffic here is crap as per

usual, but, all in all, I've missed Boston. And you and Laurie, of course," he added with a dry grin.

His dad gestured to the living room and took a seat on the white leather sofa. "Well, your sister and I appreciate that. It's partly why I changed your territory. I assume you know the other reason."

Jack sat, too. Anticipation coursed through him as soon as his father mentioned business. *This is it*, he thought. The national sales manager position had opened up, and now with his father's health not what it used to be, the time was growing closer to pass the baton.

He leaned forward, friction barely keeping him in his seat, but he willed himself to stay in control. "I know exactly why you changed it," he stated evenly.

"Good."

"I'll take it."

His father paused, deep lines creasing his forehead. "What exactly will you be taking?"

"The national sales manager position. I'll take it."

Leonard blew out a long breath, drumming his fingers on the arm of the sofa in a nervous gesture that made Jack grow wary. "I don't know how to tell you this, but I've decided not to give you that promotion. At least for now."

Jack almost fell off the sofa. "What are you talking about? How can I ever take over as president some day if I don't make this move up in the company now?"

His father's sudden silence had him breaking into a cool sweat between the blades of his shoulders. Jack narrowed his eyes. "I *am* going to take over this company someday, aren't I?"

Leonard cleared his throat. "You might be getting ahead

of yourself."

"Ahead of myself? The position just became available. Plus, I'm your son."

"True. But I could easily give the job to Laurie," his father countered.

Jack knew that wasn't going to happen. As much as he loved his sister, she wasn't the type to run a company. Besides having no financial education whatsoever, she loved being a stay-at-home mom and having her house to run. "Come on, Dad, you have to start training me to take over."

"There's nothing I would like better than for you to take over for me someday," his father stated in a somewhat reassuring tone, "but I think you still need a little maturing."

Jack stared at him blankly. "Maturing? I'm thirty-four years old."

"Now, that's just a number," his father said with a chuckle. "Nothing else."

"What are you talking about then?"

His dad's expression quickly sobered. "Well, the stockholders seem to have some…*issues* with your reputation and how it could affect the company in the long run."

"My reputation? There are no problems with my reputation. I'm your number-one wholesaler on the East Coast."

"Yes, but the stockholders have more of an issue with your, ah, *personal* reputation. In short, you change women like you change underwear. I happen to agree."

"*What?*" Jack shot out of his seat and began pacing the room. He reached up and roughly worked loose his tie, which now felt like a hangman's noose around his neck. "That's ridiculous. But even if it were true, it's my *personal* life. That has no effect on my business life."

"Well, when your personal life becomes front-page news, it does have an effect," Leonard said, sweeping his arm in the direction of the coffee table where the recent issue of *Boston* magazine lay.

Jack winced. "You, uh, saw that article, huh?"

"Yes, and I'm sure the board saw it too. The single life may be all fun and games to you, but to them, instability in your personal life translates to instability at work. Managing a company is like managing one giant relationship. And *you*, my dear boy, according to that article, have never been in a relationship longer than a month."

"That's not…" *Is it true?* He gave it some thought. He had just broken up with Brianna before he was asked to do the interview. Then before that there was Rachel. Then Mila. Giselle. Hmm…perhaps there was a grain of truth in there somewhere.

His father sighed tiredly. "That's what I thought."

Jack rubbed a hand over his face. "I don't understand any of this. If you have no plans to promote me, then I'm not sure what I'm doing here."

"Being closer to your family was something I thought would be nice for you, Jack. I even entertained the idea you'd *like* to be home again."

Jack looked away. A part of him *had* only agreed to come back because he thought he was going to get that promotion. And now, he'd turned his life upside down for nothing. "I do like being home again. It's not that, but—"

"Maybe you could even find a nice girl and settle down here now. Sabrina Cassidy—"

"Sabrina Cassidy?" He didn't mean to snap at his dad, but just the sound of that woman's name had his blood

pressure skyrocketing. "What does she have to do with anything?"

Sabrina was one of the internal wholesalers at Brenner Capital, which meant she worked as an assistant to one of the senior wholesalers who, like himself, did the actual traveling to brokerage firms. She was an excellent worker but the kind of woman who thought she was always right. Jack had even secretly dubbed her "Little Miss Perfect." Unfortunately, most times she *was* right, which was one of the reasons why his father adored her. Jack, however, did not share that feeling.

His father raised his eyebrows. "I wasn't going to suggest you settle down with her—although you could do worse."

"Well, forget it. She's engaged already anyway."

"Rumor has it she's not engaged anymore. But someone as smart and hardworking as she is would be a huge step up from the supermodel airheads you seem so accustomed to parading around with. It wouldn't hurt to look for a woman with some family sensibilities. You know, I would like grandchildren someday," he added with a smile.

"You already have grandchildren."

His father's jaw tightened. "Not from *you*."

Jack heaved a frustrated sigh. He hated to burst his father's bubble, but it had to be said. "Look, Dad, I'm sorry, but I'm not going to suddenly get married and have kids just because it will look good to the board and will somehow make me a better executive. Not going to happen. Plus, I don't have time for a family. It's not in me. I like—no, *love*—the way things are right now." He'd given that life up to move back here. He paused and grinned without guile. "I'd love it even more if I was the National Sales manager."

"There's more to life than this company."

Jack remained silent. There was no use arguing about it. He wasn't about to change his father's or the stockholders' minds, so it seemed a moot point.

"Jack, no one is forcing you to get married. But I think there are other ways—like keeping your personal life out of the spotlight, for one—that could highly influence them. You know how conservative they are in their values. Once I'm convinced you're ready to get serious and start acting like a responsible man, I can go to the stockholders and we can talk again about that promotion. Fair enough?"

Jack stared at his father. Just like that, he felt as if he were a teenager who broke the neighbor's window with a baseball and now had to figure out how to make amends. It was humiliating, to say the least. He was a grown man—and dammit, he already was a responsible man. "Dad, you have to hear me out. I think if you went to the board now and—"

His dad raised a spread hand. "I don't want to hear anything else from you. Go out there and *show* me instead."

Knowing all too well his father's adamant look, Jack wisely shut his mouth. Without a glance back, he stormed out of the penthouse.

Great. Just great. He came back to town and the first thing that happened was his personal life going under a microscope.

There's more to life than this company.

No. Not for him there wasn't. Work filled Jack's life and had never let him down through all these years. He couldn't give up on it now. It was his lifeblood. But he needed this company not only for himself, he also needed it for his father. Jack had already failed his mom. He couldn't fail his dad, too.

Jack hadn't realized how his reputation with women had preceded him—or that it would be perceived as something bad. Women were a weakness to him, but not so much that he couldn't change. He could. He *had* to. Desperation was not an emotion he was used to feeling, and he didn't like it one bit. Who knew what his father's health was really like? The board could even force him to retire early. Time could be running out. Jack needed to change people's opinion of him. And fast.

Perhaps his father had a point. Maybe it was time for him to settle down and…

No. The thought made him queasy, but it also made him wonder. Maybe he could convince his father and the stockholder board to reconsider quicker than he originally thought if it *looked* like he was ready to settle down. All he needed to do was find himself a nice, girl-next-door type of girlfriend.

Or at least a fake one.

Chapter Two

Sabrina spent a good fifteen minutes searching her kitchen cabinets for coffee and almost wailed when the only thing she came up with was chamomile tea. How was this possible? She usually had a perfect methodology to her grocery shopping. Yet somehow her organization and timing had failed her. Monday morning and she was completely out of coffee. Talk about bad luck.

For a split second she actually entertained the idea of going to the third floor of her apartment building and borrowing some from David. Having her fiancé living above her had been extremely convenient when they were dating. A little awkward now that they were broken up—even if temporarily.

But she figured going up there could accomplish two things: 1) she could get the coffee she so desperately needed and 2) she could ever so casually bring up the topic of seeing him with that woman on Saturday night and find out who she was. Just to make sure she understood where things stood between them.

It seemed like a good plan until she glanced at the clock. At seven thirty in the morning, David would already be at the hospital. So she went with her next, if not always reliable, option: her landlady, Mrs. Metzger.

Sabrina walked two doors down and knocked. Mrs. Metzger wasted no time and quickly stood opposite her with a wrinkled nose and an almost pained expression. "Honey, a little eye shadow would do wonders for you," she said in way of greeting.

Sabrina brought a hand up to her face. She'd forgotten she hadn't put on any makeup yet. "I'll get right on that. But in the meantime, do you have any coffee I could borrow? I'm, uh, kind of desperate here."

Helen Metzger lived alone with her cat, Theo. The woman was attractive and in good shape for sixty-eight, if you could get past the high platinum beehive hairstyle and the George Hamilton tan. Her husband had been in real estate and had owned various properties along the north shore area. When he had passed away almost five years ago, she had sold them all, except for this one apartment complex in the old shore town of Swampscott. The woman had grown children of her own, but she'd recently appointed herself Sabrina's surrogate mother when she'd heard how Sabrina had grown up never knowing her parents.

"Oh heavens, no," Mrs. Metzger said, laying a spread hand over her heart. "Never touch the stuff. Palpitations," she whispered.

Sabrina's shoulders slumped. Strike two. Her day was on quite a roll. "Okay, thanks anyway, Mrs. Metzger."

She was about to turn away, but her landlady grabbed her arm. "Hold on, hon." The older woman looked around anxiously, then licked her bright pink stained lips. "I need a favor."

"A favor?"

"I'm having the apartment painted this weekend, and I was wondering if Theo and I could stay with you while it's being done. Those paint fumes give me terrible migraines."

"Oh, uh…" It's not as if Sabrina didn't like the woman. In fact, Mrs. Metzger was one of the few friends, besides David, that she had in the building. But she was a bit eccentric. "Why don't you stay with one of your sons?" she asked.

Mrs. Metzger looked appalled at the idea. "Are you kidding? The holidays are coming up soon enough as it is. That will give me all the family time I can stand for the next couple of months."

"At least you have a family to spend the holidays with," she murmured, feeling that familiar sickness settle in her stomach.

Mrs. Metzger patted her arm. "I'm sorry, hon, I wasn't thinking. But if you knew my little devil grandchildren, you'd understand."

The truth was Sabrina would never understand. Her landlady's attitude toward her sons was unfathomable. Sabrina would give anything to have a family. Growing up, she had been placed in some very nice foster homes, but in the end it never seemed to matter. Just when she was starting to grow attached to them, she'd be plucked out and moved to another family. After a while, she'd closed off her heart to them. It hurt too much to be abandoned like that over and over again. Always alone. Unconnected. Unloved. Even when she tried so hard to be perfect. She didn't think she could survive if she lost David now, too. Not when she was so close to finally having it all.

Sabrina's vision blurred with unshed tears, but she quickly blinked them away. "Of course you can stay with me," she told the woman. "David won't be coming by anyway. He's been keeping himself pretty busy lately."

The older woman nodded sympathetically. "I know."

She frowned. "What do you mean?"

"I know *exactly* how he's been keeping busy. I saw the doctor and his new friend the other night."

"Really? When? Did they go up to his apartment?"

The woman pursed her lips in thought. "Briefly."

"Oh, well, that must have been business then." She hoped.

Mrs. Metzger patted Sabrina's shoulder. "Look, I was thinking, why don't you spend Thanksgiving with the boys and me? I mean, just in case you haven't made up with David by then."

"Thank you, Mrs. Metzger, but no thank you. I'm sure I'll be spending Thanksgiving with his family."

"You know, hon, not all men are like my Wally. Some men are never ready to settle down."

"Oh, David is," she stressed. She and David would talk for hours about what their children would look like and where they would live someday. Surely a man who wasn't ready for marriage wouldn't bring up topics like that. "But most of all, he loves me," she added.

That was no assumption. David did love her. He told her he did whenever he spoke to her, even since their separation. So why wouldn't she hold out hope that they'd eventually get back together?

The woman shrugged. "If that's what'll make you happy."

Sabrina smiled, remembering the words of Madame Butterfly and clinging to them like a life preserver. "Don't worry. Everything will work out in the end. You'll see. David and I being together is…fate."

Sabrina's smile faded as she turned away and walked back into her empty apartment. It seemed so lifeless with David's things gone. No more of his ties carelessly hung over the back of her chairs after he'd come straight to her place after work. His lumbar back pillow he needed whenever they watched TV together wasn't taking up room on her sofa anymore. He'd even taken back his Keurig coffee machine. The only reminder she had of him was his niece's guinea pig. Sophia started suffering with terrible allergies not long after she got him, so Sabrina offered to take care of him for her. He wasn't much company as far as pets went, but he was better than nothing.

She had to remind herself that David had only been gone a month. Not that long, yet to her, it seemed like years. Maybe she was foolish to wait for him. But he was still everything she ever wanted—stable, family-oriented, handsome, kind.

She walked over to her coffee table and picked up the only picture she had of her parents. She studied their smiling faces and wished she could remember them. They had died in an automobile accident when she was very young. But she had a feeling they still watched over her, even in some small way had a hand in her meeting David. After all, there were too many coincidences to ignore.

Sabrina placed the picture back down and fingered the

crystal clover pendant she always wore for luck, hoping they'd give her another sign soon. She had told Mrs. Metzger that she and David being together was fate, and that wasn't a lie. She believed it wholeheartedly. But, then again, she had to.

Because the idea of ending up alone was something far less imaginable.

• • •

Brenner Capital Investments was located on the thirty-second floor in One Financial Center, adjacent to Dewey Square in Boston. It consisted of a sizeable open space of about twenty desks where internal wholesalers sat and answered telephones or emailed questions about their mutual fund products and assisted the senior wholesalers who were out traveling on the road to the actual brokerage firms. Several private offices were on hand for wholesalers in the area to use when they weren't traveling, and, of course, there was a huge private office for the founder and chairman of the firm, Mr. Leonard W. Brenner.

As Sabrina approached her desk, she glanced over at her girlfriend, Christine Young, and had to suppress a laugh. Chris's desk looked as if somebody declared war on it, and her thin blond hair was already half out of her hair clip. Unfortunately, Chris looked as she always did first thing in the morning—like her day had just ended.

"Good morning," Sabrina called out.

Chris beamed at her and made her way over. "You're saying that now. Wait until you check your email."

Sabrina frowned at her computer. Why did the higher-ups

wait to drop bombs on Mondays? "I can't look. Just tell me."

"Brace yourself."

Sabrina placed her hands on her desk. "Officially braced."

"Jack Brenner has been transferred back to Boston. He's in the corner office now."

Sabrina groaned even though she was hardly surprised at the news. When the national sales manager position opened up, she had assumed Jack would be given the job. All Jack had to do was go to Daddy and he'd be given anything he wanted. The man never followed protocol. He never paid his dues as an internal wholesaler first as everyone else had. He was automatically placed as senior above those who'd worked longer in the company. And now the spoiled prodigy son was back, expecting everyone to bow down before him.

"Thanks for the warning. I'll avoid that area. Wouldn't want to poke a sleeping bear this early in the day."

Chris chuckled. "Yes, you do have a way of getting under each other's skin. Hey, listen, before I forget, Joe's side of the family is *forcing* me to have Thanksgiving this year, so if you want to hang out with our crazy family, you're more than welcome."

Sabrina sighed. "This split between David and me is temporary." She inwardly cringed at her own words. That statement was getting old fast, and it sounded less and less convincing the more she said it. "David said he just needed some space to make sure we were making the right decision. It was completely mutual." *Sort of.*

"Well, of course it is, but I just want to give you options." Chris glanced over Sabrina's shoulder and her eyes went wide. "Uh-oh, poked bear at twelve o'clock. And he's coming our way."

Sabrina clamped her lips together and resisted the urge to look. Jack Brenner probably couldn't wait to gloat over his new promotion. That had to be the reason he was even gracing them with his presence.

"Good morning, ladies," Jack said as he approached. "Ah, Sabrina, I've been looking for you."

Of course you have. The last thing she wanted to do was make chitchat with Jack Brenner, but she forced herself to turn around. As soon as she did, he hit her with that devastating grin he no doubt had been using to unravel women since puberty, and her knees did an odd little wobble.

Well. She obviously wasn't as immune to Jack's good looks as she'd thought. He was a head taller than her and could fill a suit as if he'd been born in one. His cropped brown hair was gelled with a little flip in the front, giving him that leading-man kind of aura that the girls in the office loved to gush over. Jack smelled as enticing as he looked, too—like shampoo and spice—and a little shiver of awareness passed through her. Then she remembered to breathe.

Get a grip, Sabrina.

His blue eyes seared through her, but she wouldn't give him the satisfaction of showing even an ounce of reaction. Lucky for her she was in love with someone else. She could easily see how other women could fall for such superficial charms as his.

"Congratulations," she offered, beating him to the punch.

His dark brows furrowed. "Congratulations?"

Oh, he was good. Milking every last drop like that. Fine. Since he was now her boss, she'd play along. "Yes, congratulations on being named national sales manager. I assume that's what you came over to tell us."

She mentally prepared herself, ready for the arrogance that would be plastered all over his face. But instead, his confidence looked shaken. "Actually, no. I came over because I wanted to talk to you. In private," he added, glancing at Chris.

Chris took the hint and made a thumb gesture behind her. "Right. I have to go make some phone calls anyway."

Sabrina folded her arms, knowing Jack wasn't the type to mince words or waste time. Especially if that time was his. "What's so important you want to talk to me about, *boss*?"

He leaned in and lowered his voice. "You can cut the congratulations and the boss crap. For your information, I didn't get the national sales manager position."

Now she was surprised. "But I thought—"

"Yeah. I know." His forehead wrinkled in a frown. "Me too."

She studied Jack and for a second, she almost felt sorry for him. She knew how much he'd wanted that position. Everybody knew. Then she remembered how she was passed over for the Connecticut wholesaler position because Jack had wanted it, and that moment of sympathy passed just as quickly as it came. He could charm any woman and had everyone in the company eating out of his hand merely because he was Leonard Brenner's son. But it obviously took a lot more than connections to get the board of directors to give him that coveted position. Did it make her a bad person that she felt some satisfaction that the Boy Wonder finally didn't get what he wanted?

Still, good manners compelled her to say something encouraging. "I'm sorry, Jack. I know how it feels when things don't go according to plan."

"Yeah, I'm sorry too," he said, gesturing to her bare engagement finger.

She stuffed her hands in her pockets and lifted her chin. She didn't know why, but Jack Brenner knowing anything about her personal life rankled her more than it should have, and as a result she felt an overpowering need to save face. "You heard wrong. I am still engaged. In fact, we'll be setting a wedding date soon. *Very* soon."

"Oh. My mistake. I wish you both lots of luck then."

"Thanks, we'll need that luck. After all, we all can't be *you*." She lifted an eyebrow in challenge. "Number three on *Boston* magazine's Top Ten list of Bachelors? Wow, that's quite an accomplishment. How do you do it?"

Those full lips of his curved in amusement. "Well, you know what Walt Disney said: 'All our dreams can come true—if we have the courage to pursue them.'"

"That and I'm sure the breakup with—what was that actress's name? Gazelle?—moved you up the list."

"Her name is Giselle." His eyes narrowed dangerously. "So you're the one who told my father about that. I knew you had it in for me. That move cost me the promotion."

She snorted. "Oh, please. I didn't have to tell him anything about what's-her-boobs. He has eyes."

He shook his head with a laugh. "You are the most uptight woman I've ever met."

"You're the most arrogant man *I've* ever met."

"Who are you calling arro—"

The door to Mr. Brenner's office swung open. Her boss's expression was curious—and a bit cautious—as he stepped out and noticed them both standing there with fingers pointed in each other's face.

"Ah, good," he said, a smile growing on his lips. "Jack must have already told you the news."

Sabrina blinked. "News?"

Jack cleared his throat. "Actually, no, I was just getting to that."

"You were just getting to what?" she asked.

Mr. Brenner came alongside Jack and placed a hand on his shoulder. "I've moved Jack back home. He'll now be covering the territory of Massachusetts up through Maine. Felicia Wilson will now cover Connecticut and New York."

A fog began to swirl in her head as she pieced together that information. "But I worked with Felicia. That means…" Her gaze slowly traveled to Jack.

Jack actually had the nerve to look like he was enjoying himself. "You'll be working with *me*."

Oh, crud.

Mr. Brenner smiled at her. "I knew you wouldn't have a problem with the switch."

Sabrina's world spun as she stared at her boss. She could see the family resemblance now. Father and son standing side by side, she noticed how they both had the same square jaw and deep-set eyes, although Mr. Brenner's eyes were more of a baby blue and nowhere near the ice color of Jack's. One other difference was a bit more obvious, though. Where Mr. Brenner's mouth wore a gentle, pleasant expression, his son's smirk said he was a man who enjoyed pushing the envelope. Jack was going to be hell to work with.

Double crud.

"No, that's absolutely fine," she choked out. And it would be fine.

If she had a lobotomy.

"Good," Mr. Brenner said with a nod. "I knew I could count on you. You'll make a great team." Then with a pointed look at his son, he turned around and disappeared back into his office.

Jack stepped closer to her, making a *tsk-tsk* sound. "Gee, the 'it's going to be nice to work with you' speech I had planned just seems awkward now."

She cut him a sharp look. "Please. I know you don't like this any better than I do."

"That's not necessarily true. We may not get along personally, but professionally I can admire many of your fine assets."

"Keep your eyes off my assets."

His simmering smile returned. "Touchy."

"You won't be doing any of that, either."

He sighed and looked away, over her head. "You know, Sabrina, contrary to those newspaper and magazine articles you've read about me, I don't have a one-track mind."

Sabrina wanted to retort with something childish and insulting, but figured she'd pressed her luck with him enough. Jack Brenner may not be her boss, but he was her boss's son. And now, her business partner. Time to rise above her dislike. She would have to suck it up and play nice. But considering it was Monday morning and she hadn't any caffeine yet, she allowed herself one last cheap parting shot.

"As long as you remember that, *playboy*, we'll get along just fine."

Then, not trusting herself in Jack's presence any longer, she walked away in search of her sanity—and a good, strong cup of coffee.

Chapter Three

With warring feelings of frustration and admiration, Jack watched Sabrina storm off. He had to hand it to her. No other person in this company would ever have the nerve to go toe-to-toe with him like that. Although, he didn't have a good feeling about what that meant with regards to his partnership with her. His dad had to have made a huge mistake.

The door to his father's office opened again. "Sabrina, I—" Leonard Brenner looked up from the papers in his hand and frowned. "Oh. Where did Sabrina go?"

Jack shrugged. "She mentioned something about coffee."

"Fine. Tell her I want to talk to her when she gets back."

"Dad, wait. Are you sure this is a good idea about Sabrina and me? Maybe she'd be better off staying as Felicia's internal assistant?"

Leonard pushed his glasses up the bridge of his nose and blew out an impatient breath. "No. Sabrina's too good a worker for Felicia. I'd like to see how she functions without her. When I said you and she would make a good team, I meant it. She's just the partner you need if you're serious about doing well in this company."

Jack straightened. "I am. You know that."

"Good. Now's the time to take a break from those late-night parties and start spending those nights getting to know the territory. Sabrina can help you with that."

"Yes, sir."

Jack turned away and headed to his desk. Well, it looked as if he was stuck with Little Miss Perfect. Great. He supposed he could put their mutual dislike aside and work it out with her. After all, he was a professional and had always thought Sabrina was quick and smart. She definitely had ample in the spunk department. And—if he was being completely honest with himself—she wasn't hard to look at, either.

Sure, he could admit Sabrina was pretty in a natural kind of way, if you were a sucker for that soft blue, sloe-eyed look, or happen to have a Snow White fetish. Not someone *he* would ever get involved with. She was a little high strung and prim for his taste. *Probably needs to cut down on the caffeine*, he thought gruffly. Of course, Sabrina had the power to make work miserable for him. Which meant his *life* would be miserable—since his life was his work.

How could he look responsible to his father and to the board if his very own partner thought he was too much of a player to be considered good for the company?

That magazine article certainly confirmed whatever opinion Sabrina had already made about him, and if she felt that way, it was no wonder the stockholders felt the same. As much as he hated to admit it, he needed Sabrina Cassidy on his side for more than just their working relationship. His father respected her. And if she could change her opinion of Jack, it would go a long way in changing others' opinions too. He thought about that, then headed to the elevators, suddenly in the mood for a cup of coffee too.

Sabrina wasn't a woman to be charmed into reconsideration. No, he'd have to appeal to her more logical side. Although with the way she'd completely shut him down, he doubted he'd ever find it. Or that she'd even let him close enough to try.

But if he wanted to save his reputation, that was exactly what he was going to have to do.

. . .

Sabrina stood in line at the first-floor coffee shop and rubbed her pounding head. She should have called in sick. If she had bothered to check her horoscope today, she was sure it would have told her the same thing.

Shifting her stance, she craned her neck to see the front of the line. Apparently the entire east end of Boston went out for coffee at nine forty-five in the morning. Lucky her. That only added to her tension. Jack Brenner and his blue I'm-too-sexy-for-my-face eyes were the main cause.

The Playboy was now her partner. Wonderful. She hoped future correspondence with him would be minimal— and if there was a God, through email only. First problems with David and now problems with work. Could her week get any worse?

Glancing out the window, she caught sight of a familiar head of blond hair. Forgetting about her need for caffeine, she jumped out of line and ran to the large window overlooking the street. With hands and face pressed against the glass, she watched as David strolled down the sidewalk with that same redhead from Saturday night. With each step they took, a little piece of her heart broke off and shattered.

He looks happy, she thought miserably, then watched him cock his head to say something in the woman's ear. Sabrina wished she could have heard what he said, because whatever it was caused the redhead to shove at him and burst into exaggerated laughter.

Sabrina's heart dropped accordingly. She couldn't remember David saying anything so funny when *they* were together. Since when had he become such a comedian? Her throat ached in defeat as she continued to watch them. What she wanted her ideal life to be flashed before her eyes and fizzled into a massive puff of red-haired smoke.

"You look like you've lost your best friend."

Sabrina jumped, even though the words were said soft and low. Pushing herself away from the window, she glanced up into Jack Brenner's handsome face.

"What are we staring at?" With amused eyes, he leaned his body in and looked out the window for himself. His expression quickly sobered. "Ah, I see," he said with a nod. "Trouble in paradise?"

"What are you doing here?" she spat, trying to keep her lower lip from quivering.

Stupid Jack Brenner was showing up at the worst possible time. The last thing she wanted was for him to see her cry. But loneliness—her archenemy and best friend—wound its way inside her chest and squeezed hard.

He looked down at her, and his eyes grew concerned.

"Actually, I wanted to buy you a coffee. Although"—he reached out and captured a strand of her hair, resting it gently behind her ear—"it looks as if you could use something a little stronger."

Seeing David with that woman again and Jack's uncharacteristically sympathetic gesture was her complete undoing. Without warning, she burst into tears.

"Hey, hey," he said, sounding alarmed. He gave her a few stiff pats on the back. "Oh no. No, no. Please don't cry."

She crumbled further. His words only made her cry harder.

Jack quickly gathered her in his arms and led her out the door. "Let's go get some air," he suggested.

"I don't want air," she mumbled into his starched shirt.

"Don't tell that to your lungs."

They walked outside and sat down on a nearby bench. Jack still had her nestled into his chest. She could hear people walking the sidewalks around her and the rush of traffic on the street. The wind picked up and blew the back of her hair, making her shiver. She hated to admit it, but being outside did make her feel a little better.

Jack loosened his grip but didn't let go of her. "You okay?"

"I'm sorry," she said, her head still buried in his shirt. "I'm so sorry. I'm usually more in control than this."

"Believe me, I know." She heard laughter in his voice. "But I do have a sister, and according to her, it's okay to have breakdowns now and again."

No. She rarely had breakdowns. She prided herself on always staying in control, keeping her emotions on an even keel. That was how she survived her time in the foster care system. It was better than showing her hurt, especially since no one was ever there to reach for her if she had. Even when David suggested their split, she'd held in her heartache and amicably agreed. She'd tried to be perfect, what David wanted. Turned out, he didn't want her at all.

Sniffling, she squirmed out of Jack's arms. She slid her gaze upward. He had mascara smudges on his shirt, which meant she probably looked like a raccoon. Or worse, the Hamburglar. Her eyes began to fill up again.

Jack held out his hands like a crossing guard. "It's okay to have breakdowns, only within reason."

She let out a watery chuckle. Jack was, unfortunately, right. She could pull it together. She had to.

She took a deep breath and let it out slowly, feeling the near-hysteria drift away. "Yes, you're right. I'm fine." When Jack just stared at her, she smoothed out her skirt and added, "I am. Thank you."

"Okay, then talk to me. I guess I correctly assumed that was your fiancé. Tell me what happened."

Her face heated. Oh, crap. She must look in worse shape than she thought if Jack was trying to play Dr. Phil. She just shook her head.

"Okay, then how about a clue," he said. "Two words? One syllable?"

Her embarrassment quickly turned to annoyance. She swiped at her eyes and sniffled. "Look, Jack, I'm sorry, but I really don't want to talk about this with you. No offense."

"None taken," he said, brushing at the makeup stains on his shirt. "But we are partners now and as hard as it is for you to believe, I am trying to be a nice guy here."

Sabrina studied him, weighing his words. Yes, Jack was

being a nice guy. She honestly hadn't known he had it in him. With the way he was looking at her, she was beginning to think that maybe he didn't have an ulterior motive. He patiently sat with her like he had all the time in the world to listen to her problems.

Then he smiled—and not one of those smug smiles he'd been giving out like candy since she first laid eyes on him. This one was a gentle smile—comforting—and just enough to twist something deep inside her.

"I lied," she blurted.

His brows rose. "Lied?"

She nodded, her shoulders slumping. "Those rumors you heard about my engagement are true. I'm not…that is… My fiancé and I have decided to—to take a step back and evaluate our relationship." She held up her left hand. "Hence the missing ring."

"I see."

"Everyone thinks David has more than just cold feet. And well, maybe that's true, but to be honest, I really thought we'd be back together by now. Even Madame Butterfly said the same thing."

Jack looked at her blankly. "Madame Butterfly. Well, I'm sure anyone with a name like that *has* to be in the know."

She crossed her arms. To Jack it probably seemed ridiculous for someone like her, who surrounded herself in control and structure, to believe in psychics and superstitions. But it gave her a strange comfort and even hope that she had control over her fate as well. "I'm serious here."

"I was afraid of that," he muttered. "Look, if there's one thing I've learned in business it's that you can't wait for… the *Madame Butterflies* of the world for things to naturally occur. Success comes down to going after what you want yourself. Do you want to be a success?"

"Yes," she said warily.

"And do you want David back?"

"Well, of course," she huffed. "I would do anything to get him back."

He sat back, raising an eyebrow as he studied her. "Anything?"

"Yes, anything. I love him."

"Interesting," he said, more to himself than her.

She bit her lip. "I'm not sure what to do but wait, though."

Jack sat silently for a few moments looking deep in thought, and then he snapped his head up and said, "That's not good enough." His gaze didn't waver. "You need to *fight*."

"What?"

"Fight for him. And don't tell me you can't. I happen to know firsthand that you have more than enough fight in you," he said drily. "But I can help you."

She stared at him. Oh, she knew Jack was arrogant, but this? This comment completely confirmed the God complex she always suspected he had. "*You?* You would help me get my fiancé back?"

"*Ex*-fiancé," he corrected. "But yes, I would."

She narrowed her eyes and allowed her voice to dip into a warning tone. "And why would you do that?"

His lips shifted to an easy smile. "I have a deep-rooted desire to see my new partner happy and settled in her life. Is that so wrong?"

She snorted-laughed. "For you? It's very wrong. You're up to something."

He pressed a hand to his chest and rubbed, pretending to be wounded. "I'm truly hurt that you would think that I—"

"Just get to the point, Jack. What do you want in return?"

For the first time since she'd known him, Jack actually looked uncomfortable. He cleared his throat a few times before answering. "Between you and me, I didn't get that promotion because the board feels my personal life may need a makeover. Of sorts. My father unfortunately agrees."

"Mm-hmm. Not to take sides, but when your recent breakup starts trending on Twitter, your personal life might need a little reevaluating."

She had the satisfaction of seeing his eyes narrow. "Yes, well, my dad has even gone so far as to say that I should find a nice sensible girl and settle down."

"What do you want me to do? Find you a nice, normal girl to make you look respectable?" She thought about Maddie but worried that maybe she was *too* nice and sensible for him. It could be like putting a goldfish and a piranha together in a fish tank. She couldn't do that to Maddie. She couldn't do that to *any* woman she knew.

"Actually…" His gaze lingered on his clenched fists, then swung up and pinned her to her seat. "I already found the perfect girl."

Several seconds ticked by.

Realization hit her and she jumped off the bench. "Not on your *life*."

Jack grabbed her hand and pulled her back down. "Will you listen before jumping to conclusions? I'm not asking you to settle down with me for real. Just for pretend."

"You're insane," she said, shaking off his hand. "Of all

the women in Boston, why me?"

"Well, look at you," he said, pointing. She followed his finger and looked down but only saw a cream-colored turtleneck over a black wool skirt. "You're hardworking, sensible, and obviously want to get married," he continued. "Pretty much the antithesis of every woman I've dated."

"You mean because my IQ is larger than my bra size?"

His lips thinned. "I *mean* because you have my father's respect."

"I do?" She frowned, not because she was unhappy to hear that information but because she was surprised. "Then why did he pass me over for a senior wholesaling position?"

"*What?* You wanted my job?"

She waved his question away. "Never mind." She sighed, putting her head in her hands. Yes, she felt she should have gotten Jack's territory. But it didn't matter. It wasn't the time to get into work issues. Right now her priority was David.

"Sabrina, will you shove your animosity toward me away for one brief second and think about this? It would be a win-win for both of us. David thinks you're adoringly waiting in the wings, giving him as long as it takes to make up his mind."

She dropped her hands and blinked. "But he would be right."

"No, you have to change his thinking. He has to believe you've moved on. And the best way to do that is by making him think you're interested in another man. Another man who happens to be number three on New England's Top Bachelors list would be quite the coup. If David just has cold feet like you say he does, then there's nothing like good old-fashioned jealousy to warm them up again."

"That's original," she murmured.

He shrugged. "I find the classics work best."

"What would I have to do exactly?" she asked.

Jack scanned around them, then lowered his voice. "Convince everyone in the office, including my father, that we're in a serious relationship. Perhaps attend a few high-profile events with me. David has to think we're dating anyway. Pretty simple when you think about it."

Sabrina felt her stomach tighten. Nothing seemed simple at all. "How long would I have to…pretend?"

"I'm not sure. At least until the next quarterly board meeting—even if David comes back to you before then. I need to look as if I gave this relationship at least the old college try."

"I—I don't know." She began chewing on her thumbnail in thought, then cast a side glance at Jack.

David would be jealous of a man like Jack. She didn't doubt it. Jack was ridiculously good-looking. Intelligent—*mostly*. And rich. He also had the kind of wide shoulders and brawny arms that could wrap around a female wrestler and somehow make her feel as delicate as a flower. Jack certainly *seemed* the kind of man any woman would love to catch on the rebound from a broken heart. Not her, of course. She had no interest in rich, handsome playboys.

But David didn't know that.

The whole idea still sounded so wrong, so *sordid*. She doubted anyone at work would believe she and Jack would even think about dating each other. But maybe luck threw Jack in her path for a reason. Would she be a fool not to take him up on it? Was Jack part of her "journey" to David that Madame Butterfly had mentioned? She couldn't be sure.

She needed more time to think.

"It would mean a lot to me," Jack added.

She shot him a look. "Oh, gee, now there's an incentive. Why didn't you say so in the first place?"

He let out a muffled snort, but she couldn't tell if it was from laughter or frustration. He reached into his suit jacket and pulled out his wallet. He took his business card and tucked it in her palm. "My cell phone number is on the back in case you change your mind after work. Call me anytime."

"I bet you say that to all the girls," she said, batting her eyelashes.

Jack let out a slow, predatory grin that disintegrated her mocking attitude.

"No, not all the girls," he said in a silky voice. His warm hand closed over hers, and he leaned in so close she could feel his breath on her cheek. "I only say that to my *girlfriends*."

A charge of awareness raced through her. Sabrina swallowed hard, backing down her reaction. Then he stood and walked back inside the building, leaving her alone with her heartache, her loneliness, what little pride she had left, and a whole lot more to think about.

Chapter Four

Jack drummed his fingers on his desk. No doubt about it. He had completely lost his mind.

What had he been thinking when he'd asked Sabrina to pretend to be his girlfriend?

But at the time it'd made perfect sense. He was desperate for a solution to his playboy reputation and there Sabrina was, in his arms, desperate to get her ex-fiancé back. When she'd mentioned she'd do anything in that regard, his mind sprung into action and a plan was formed. He couldn't have found a better candidate if he'd placed his own personal Want Ad. She was exactly the kind of woman his father would love to see him settle down with. However, his dad didn't understand that relationships were not Jack's strong suit. Too messy. And he didn't need the complication.

Yet, he did need Sabrina Cassidy. He had little choice at this point.

But she needed him, too.

Jack had no doubt he could help her get her fiancé back, if in fact the guy loved her and simply had cold feet like she said. The real question was how much did Sabrina truly want him back? Enough to make a deal with the devil? Because that's exactly what she saw him as. A womanizing devil.

He rubbed the back of his neck and tried not to let her opinion get to him. Who cared what she thought? It shouldn't bother him at all. There were plenty of women who thought very highly of him. Other spunky women who had a determined little chin and wide baby-blue eyes too. Not that he found any of those things about her attractive.

Oh, hell. He *did* find those things attractive, especially on Sabrina Cassidy. Not that it changed anything. She was off-limits, and he had more important wants at the moment. The only thing that mattered was that she helped him get that promotion.

The ball was in her court now.

Jack huffed out a breath as he reached for the phone. He had some calls to make, maybe invite a few board members to travel with him. That way they'd be able to see firsthand what kind of job he did. Yeah, that was a good idea. It was time he followed his own advice he'd given to Sabrina. If you wanted success you couldn't wait around for it to happen—or in this case, wait around for a certain Little Miss Perfect to make up her mind. After all, there was still a good chance she'd turn him down.

And in case she did, he'd already have a plan B in action.

• • •

It had been a long day, but Mondays usually were. Luckily,

after Sabrina's embarrassing cry on Jack's shoulder—and yet another coffee run—the rest of the afternoon had gone a whole lot smoother. There were no interruptions aside from her own thoughts. She couldn't stop thinking about how she'd made a fool of herself to Jack by pouring her heart out to him. Thankfully, she hadn't seen any more of him today.

Actually, no one had.

Jack had buried himself in one of the side offices like a groundhog and still hadn't made an appearance by the time she'd left the building after six. He seemed to be trying to show his father how diligent a worker he was and how responsible he could be. A valiant effort. But as far as she was concerned, the jury was still out.

Despite the kindness he'd shown her back at the coffee shop, she still wasn't sure what to make of him. She didn't trust him. Jack apparently paid a lot of attention to outward appearances; otherwise he would have never suggested such an outlandish idea. As if she'd ever consider helping him change his reputation. She had a reputation to protect too. Besides, she doubted Jack's idea would have helped her out. David wasn't the type to be moved by jealousy. She'd have to continue to wait for David to make up his mind on his own terms and hope for the best.

After a horrendous commute home, it was dark by the time she made it to her apartment, and she was absolutely famished. She opened her drawer of menus, but before she could place an order, there was a knock at her door. Not expecting anyone, she took her time answering it. When she finally pressed her cried-sore eye to the peephole, she gasped.

"David," she said breathlessly as she threw open the door.

"Hi, baby." His smile was hesitant. "May I come in?"

Sabrina's heart practically sang with delight when she heard him call her baby. She opened the door farther, and David entered the living room. He still wore scrubs, and his blond hair was slightly ruffled. He must have just gotten back from work. Even though she was sure he was exhausted, it didn't wear on the polished veneer of his natural good looks.

This could be it. He's decided to come back. She swallowed and tried to keep the giddiness out of her voice. "What are you doing here?"

"I felt I should return your things."

"My…things?" She finally noticed a cardboard box in his hands. "What things?"

David set the box down on her coffee table and rubbed a hand over his face. "Take a look."

She cautiously peeked inside as if she thought one of those giant fake snakes would spring out at her at any second. But she would have much preferred that to what she actually saw. The box was filled with all the personal belongings she'd left in David's apartment. A crushing feeling formed in her chest as she ran her fingers over the items: a toothbrush, a tube of her favorite spice-colored lipstick, her facial moisturizer, and the James Taylor CD they'd listened to on their road trip to Vermont. But her heart sank further when she opened up a white envelope filled with various pictures of the two of them together.

It took her a moment to realize what this all meant, but she rigidly held her tears in check. Oh, gosh, he didn't want a single reminder of her. What had she done wrong?

"So this is it," she murmured.

His hazel eyes continued to focus on James Taylor's face.

"This is it…only for now."

She looked at him sharply. "David, are you breaking up with me or not?"

He walked over to her and kissed her forehead. "No, I'm not. I don't want to lose you. It's just that…I'm asking for a little more time. I know it's unfair, and you're ready for a permanent commitment, but I'm still questioning what *I'm* ready for. And now with everything going on at the hospital, I don't want to rush and screw this up for us."

Her laugh sounded strained and pitiful to her own ears. "You're already screwing this up. David, I'm trying to be patient, but please, I want you to be honest. I've seen you around the city with another woman. A pretty redhead. Is all this space you need because of her?"

"Rose?"

She held in a snort. The redhead's name was Rose. How cliché.

"Rose is a friend from the hospital," he continued. "She's a trauma nurse. You met her once. Our schedules have been coinciding lately and well, she's been a good friend to me."

"I bet," she said tightly.

He reached out and pushed her hair behind her ears. "Don't be like that, Sabrina. I can have female friends. Just because our timing seems to be off doesn't mean I want someone else."

She squeezed her eyes closed, and her heart began to feel lighter. *He doesn't want anyone else.* Thank God. He loved her. She knew it. This talk proved it. He *was* scared of commitment even though they'd been together for three years. Three *years*. But there was a chance that this woman friend could talk him out of coming back to her. What could she do? She didn't know how else to convince him they were meant to be husband and wife and that they should have a life together. She needed to think. Then her eyes sprang open as an idea struck.

Or rather, *Jack's* idea struck.

"You're right," she said with a double dose of sincerity she didn't feel. "I know exactly what you mean, what it's like to need friendship. In fact, I've been confiding in a friend at work too."

He nodded. "Chris."

She turned away, afraid her expression would give away her lie. "No, not Chris. A new wholesaler at work. Jack."

"A *man*?"

"Mmm-hmm." She glanced over her shoulder with raised eyebrows. "Oh, does that bother you?"

He cleared his throat. "Uh, no. Not at all," he said, although his voice sounded unsure.

She took that as a good sign and continued to steamroll through her plan. "I'm glad, because Jack has been an absolute treasure to me." She resisted rolling her eyes and prayed lightning would not strike. "I'd hate to give up his friendship. He's given me lots to think about and process while we've been separated. It's so funny that he happened to come into my life just as you left it."

David frowned. "Now hold on, I haven't exactly left—"

She grabbed his hand and squeezed. "Thank you for understanding."

His face fell at that, which fueled her next words. She decided to go with the final nail in the coffin. "You should probably go. Jack told me he was going to call tonight to check up on me."

David stood there, blinking adorably, as if someone had snuck up behind him and swatted him on the back of the head. "I, uh, could stay a little longer if—"

"No," she said, holding up her palm. "I don't want to interfere with your decision-making for one more minute. You said you needed time and time I will give you. It's a big step, and I want you to be sure. For both our sakes." Drumming up whatever acting skills she had in her, she gave him her most winning smile—right before she ushered him out the door.

David turned around, his finger in the air. "Sabrina, I want you to know, this isn't good-bye. And I think you're an angel for giving me this time."

A cold knot formed in her stomach. She felt like a manipulative liar. If only David knew how far from an angel she was. "Whatever is meant to be between us *will* happen," she assured him.

Then she closed the door on his confused, handsome face and hoped she wasn't making the biggest mistake of her life.

She resisted the urge to open the door again and instead turned away. That was one of the most difficult things she'd ever done. But necessary if she wanted David back for good. In her mind, Jack's suggestion to make David jealous was ridiculous, but now something in her heart felt that he could have a point, that there was hope. Maybe a little jealousy was all David needed to push him over the edge back to her. Plus, if Jack got his promotion, she stood to get Jack's territory and a promotion herself. Win-win.

Her gaze shot to the coffee table. The box of her things sat there, almost mocking her. As much as David's words reassured her, his actions spoke of something else. Time could be running out for them. That knowledge twisted inside her, and she closed her eyes.

One last thing to do.

She realized she was trembling, but she walked over to her purse and pulled out her cell phone along with Jack's business card. Idly running her fingers over his embossed name, she had to wonder if she'd lost her mind. But then again, if that were true, she really didn't have anything left to lose. She was already relying on the advice of psychics. Why not add playboys to that list as well? She sat down at the kitchen counter and punched in the number.

After a few rings, a deep voice answered. "Hello?"

She cleared her throat. "Um, hi, Jack. It's Sabrina. From work." She felt compelled to add that part in. Who knew how many women called his number on a daily basis?

"Hello, Sabrina from work. What can I do for you?" His tone sounded amused but a little cautious.

She opened her mouth but nothing came out.

"Hello? Are you still there?"

"Y-yes. Sorry." She took a deep breath, then sighed. "I just wanted to call and tell you that I've thought about your...your..."

"Proposition?" he finished.

She wrinkled her nose. That made it sound even more sordid, like she was living out a scene from her own personal *General Hospital.* "How about we just call it your *suggestion?*"

He chuckled. "Okay, and what is your thinking on the subject of my suggestion?"

"I'll do it," she said softly, then bit her lip.

"Excellent." His voice boomed through the phone, and she could practically hear his brain filing the information and formulating what to do with it. "We can talk about it more at work tomorrow and hash out a plan that suits both of us then. You and David will be back together in no time."

"That's the least of my worries right now. I'm more concerned with what you're asking in return."

"You worry too much. All I ask is for a little display of adoration in front of others and perhaps for you to keep the venom in your voice toward me to a nice nonlethal level. Trust me, posing as my girlfriend will be a cake walk." He paused, then added, "You won't be sorry, Sabrina."

Too late. She already was.

• • •

The next day, Sabrina sat in Jack's office with the anguish of a woman who had just been sentenced ten to fifteen years with no hope of parole.

"Will you relax," he told her. "You're making me anxious, and I'm never anxious." Although he *was* anxious to get their plan started, but he was also hungry. He opened his desk drawer to his new stash of beef jerky he had on hand for such an emergency and pulled some out.

Sabrina threw her hands up in the air. "Oh, great. This is so completely fitting with you. While I'm stepping into a web of lies, you're stepping into a Slim Jim."

He looked at the beef thoughtfully, then held it out to her. "I'm sensing you need this more than I do."

"I'm a vegetarian."

"Now *that* explains a lot."

Fiancé By Fate

She bristled. "That's it. Forget it. This is so stupid. We're never going to convince anyone that we *like* each other, let alone that we're dating." Shaking her head, she was on her feet before he could blink and looked about ready to high-tail it out of his office.

"Wait," he said quickly. Where was his normal finesse when it came to women? She had a way about her that brought out his worst. But she was right. If he didn't watch himself, he'd ruin everything.

"I'm sorry, Sabrina. This will work. How about we both try to keep the smart comments to a minimum?"

She sat back down but her shoulders were still stiff. "All right then. Let's just figure this plan out so I can get back to work."

Damn, there was a lot of pent-up energy going on in that tight little body of hers. It was kind of amusing to watch, especially the way she tried to quiet her hyperventilating breaths so he wouldn't notice. Call him a jerk, but he noticed. Her chest was going in and out like a runaway steam engine and it was all he could do not to stare. And he liked what he saw.

"What do you want me to do?" she asked, breaking into those thoughts. She nibbled one corner of her lip, her hair hanging loosely as she cocked her head to the side.

"Well, I…" Their gazes met and held.

Have her eyes always been that blue? Hell. He knew she was pretty, but he never realized she was *that* pretty.

He cleared his throat and reached for more beef jerky.

"You do have some sort of agenda, right?" she asked.

"Agenda?"

"A list of dos and don'ts."

He rolled his eyes. Sabrina was definitely not a play-it-by-ear kind of woman. He should have known she'd want an itemized list of how he expected her to act.

She licked her lips. "Nothing over the top, I hope. Oh, and I guess I should have mentioned this before, but I don't want to have to, uh…"

"Don't want to have to what?" he asked, popping another piece of jerky in his mouth.

"Kiss you," she finished.

Jack froze midchew, then swallowed. *"What?"*

She shifted in her chair. "I don't want to have to kiss you."

"Absolutely not. That's nonnegotiable. You *have* to kiss me. What kind of fake girlfriend are you, anyway?"

She lifted her chin. "One that doesn't believe in public displays of affection."

"That's ridiculous."

"No, it's not. Look, you're the one who wants to change your reputation. Kissing and any other type of manhandling—fake or not—in front of people is not a way to show them you're in a serious relationship. I won't be treated like all your other bimbos. We'll just have to be convincing in other ways."

Jack sat back and grunted. Little Miss Perfect had a point, as per usual. Kissing was not something they could be caught doing at work, and even if they were out on a fake date, at their age, they wouldn't be lip-locked at some restaurant. But the idea still didn't sit well with him. Who knew that he'd actually be disturbed he wouldn't be able to kiss her?

And the more he thought about how it disturbed him,

the more disturbed he became.

"So…are you okay with that?" she asked, nibbling her bottom lip.

He forced his attention away from her mouth and smiled tightly. "No problem at all."

"Good. However, I think handholding would be completely appropriate."

"Are you sure? Hand over hand or full-on fingers entwined? I don't want to look cheap."

She folded her arms and glared at him. "Can you ever be serious?"

"Can you ever *not* be serious?"

Leonard Brenner poked his head in Jack's office then and smiled at the sight of the two of them apparently having a nice company chat. "Oh, there you are, Sabrina." He smirked as he cast a sideways glance at Jack. "I don't want to interrupt anything, but I need to steal Sabrina away from you. I wanted to go over a few of the last expense reports that Chuck just emailed me."

"No problem, Mr. Brenner," she replied. "I'll go grab my notes." Looking way too happy to leave Jack's presence and not at all like a woman smitten with a potential new boyfriend, she jumped up and turned on her heel to go.

Before she could leave, Jack reached out and blocked her with his arm. "I'm sure I can count on you to handle the situation we've, uh, discussed," he reminded her pleasantly.

She gave him a long look. If he wasn't starting to know her so well, he would have completely missed the silent message she shot him that told him exactly where he could stuff their so-called situation along with all his beef jerky.

"You can count on me," she said, letting the words roll

off her tongue as sweet as maple syrup. "I'll definitely handle the situation as *I* see fit."

Jack smothered a grin as he watched her leave. Sabrina surprised him. For all her bossiness and rule-making, he liked her. Much more than he thought he ever would.

When his father turned back to Jack, it was with a pleased expression. "This is very refreshing to see."

"What is?"

"You and Sabrina getting along so well."

Jack thought about announcing his and Sabrina's fake relationship now, but he figured it would have more believability if he didn't rush things. Played it cool. Plus, there was still the outside chance his father would go to the board before their quarterly meeting without this exercise in wholesome behavioral CEO standards.

"Yes, Sabrina is proving to be a very valuable coworker," he agreed. "It was a good decision pairing her up with me." *For more reasons than you know.*

"I'm glad you think so. I also wanted to tell you that I won't be around this afternoon."

"Why? What's going on?"

"I have to go to the doctor's."

Jack felt as if he'd taken a punch to the stomach, which made it hard for him not to sound alarmed. "Dad, are you feeling—"

"I'm fine. Just a follow-up visit with my primary-care doctor. I think he might change my meds around, but other than that, no cause for alarm."

"If you need me to come with you, I'll cancel my appointments."

"I know you would, and I appreciate it. But your sister is

going to take me." He nudged Jack with his elbow. "I get to see my grandkids that way," he said, grinning.

Jack couldn't smile back. He was too concerned about his dad's health. He wanted to do anything he could to help his dad, to be there for him. Jack hadn't been there for his mom before she died. He'd been away at college and had come home only on major holidays. If only he'd been around more, paid attention, he would have seen how lonely she was, how much she'd been hurting. If he had, he couldn't help thinking that she might not have taken her own life.

Leonard placed a comforting hand on Jack's shoulder. "Don't let my health distract you. Everything's fine."

"But I think if the board knew of your health issues they might force you to step down. You have to reconsider me for national sales manager and not wait."

"We'll see. Since you're my son, I'd like to believe you're looking to settle down, but the stockholders will need to see proof. After all, old habits do die hard." His father frowned, then motioned to the beef jerky on his desk. "You still eat that junk?"

"Um, yeah." Jack hastily swept the beef into a drawer and shrugged. "One habit to overcome at a time."

• • •

Sabrina finished the last of her reports, then sat back, trying to work out the kinks in her neck. She'd been looking at her computer screen for the past hour without a break. Unfortunately, whenever she wasn't working, her thoughts went straight to Jack.

How in the world was she going to convince people

that she and Jack were dating? They couldn't even agree on something as simple as food. More importantly, how was she going to convince David she was interested in a man like Jack?

What had she gotten herself into?

Biting her lip, she decided to take a peek at Jack's traveling schedule—just to get an idea of how often he'd be around. She called it up on her computer, and her eyes widened in surprise. Next week was jam-packed with office visits in northern Massachusetts and southern New Hampshire. Jack even had a lunch appointment for every day but Friday. Tension seeped a little from her shoulders. For someone who had the reputation of playing hard, he certainly seemed to work hard, too. Jack was taking his new territory by the horns.

Her eyes shot to Mr. Brenner's door as she heard it open. "Sabrina," he said, taking off his glasses, "I wanted to have a word with you before I left for the day."

"Of course, sir."

He paused and smiled down at her. "I know it's a little soon to ask, but I wanted to know how everything was working out with you and Jack?"

If you only knew. "Great." She beamed.

He cocked his head. "Really? I know he may be a little rough around the edges."

Ha. No kidding. But she kept silent and waited for him to continue.

"He's used to getting his own way. After his mom died, I may have let him run a little wild. His sister was just a young teenager then, so I had a lot on my plate. I didn't have it in me to rein Jack in like I should have." He shook his head.

The strings of her heart tugged, but only for the older man standing before her. "Don't worry, Mr. Brenner. Jack's really been working hard," she said soothingly. "His schedule is booked solid. It's been an absolute pleasure to team up with him. In fact, I'm seeing a whole new side of him that anyone in this company would admire."

Did those words really just come out of my mouth?

His face brightened. "Thank you, Sabrina. Keep up the good work," he said as he walked out the door.

She smiled at his retreating back and took a deep breath. Okay, that hadn't been so hard. And it wasn't much of a twist of the truth either. See? She could do this. About to go back to her computer, she heard a throat clearing. Something told her it was Jack even before she fully turned around and looked.

When she did, there he was, giving her an enthusiastic thumbs-up. That and the devilish grin plastered all over his face told her he had heard everything she had just said about him. Heat flooding her cheeks, she spun away.

Good, she thought, pummeling the keys on her computer. She was glad he'd heard. It showed she was keeping her end of the bargain. Now let's see what he could do to help her get David back.

Her phone rang. Grateful for the reprieve, Sabrina swiftly answered it. Her landlady's voice was on the other end.

"Oh, hon, I'm glad I caught you before you left for lunch." Mrs. Metzger sounded out of breath and anxious— or at least more anxious than normal.

"Is there a problem?" *Or fire or theft or pipes bursting with water as we speak?*

"I just ran into your David."

That was much worse. "You did?"

"I misjudged the boy. He spoke very highly of you."

"He did?" *Why am I so surprised?* Of course he did. He'd just told her last night that he didn't want anyone else.

"*Very* highly," Mrs. Metzger added.

Silence fell between them for several long seconds, and Sabrina was left sitting on the edge of her seat. "*And…?*" she prompted.

"They've started to paint this afternoon, so I let myself into your place and will be staying tonight."

"Huh?" Sabrina had totally forgotten she had agreed to let her landlady stay with her, but that wasn't the information she was dying to hear. "That's fine," she replied, trying to control the edge in her voice. "But Mrs. Metzger, what else about *David*?"

"Oh yes." The woman chuckled. "I thought you might be interested in learning that despite all he said about you, he's taking that friend of his to dinner tonight." She seemed to pause for dramatic effect. "At the Ram's Horn."

"The *Ram's Horn*?" Sabrina cried. She glanced around the room to make sure no one had heard her outburst. That was *their* favorite restaurant. The restaurant where David had proposed to her. How could he?

"Are you sure?" she asked. "Maybe you're mistaken."

"I'm old, hon, but not deaf."

"It's just I'm surprised…" Sabrina shifted and cradled the phone closer. That's when she saw Jack moving across the main office with the coordination and grace of an athlete in his prime. The women he passed on the way to the mail room were practically waving their pom-poms in gratitude. It gave her an idea.

"Oh, Mrs. Metzger, I could kiss you for this information!" she exclaimed, her eyes still focused on Jack.

"Hon, you're taking this better than I thought."

Sabrina was too wrapped up in formulating her plan to explain. "I have to go," she told her. "But thanks again." She hung up and glanced at the time. Almost two o'clock. She had time to get ready if she rushed home right after work. She would wear that black-and-white number she'd bought last week on Newbury Street. David hadn't seen her in it yet. Studying Jack again, she figured he could just go as he was.

Jack was perfectly put-together in his navy-blue suit and bold crimson silk necktie. She wondered what David would think when he saw him. Jack definitely looked the part of the elegant new boyfriend. He stopped to talk to her friend Chris, and Sabrina's gaze was automatically drawn to that slow, lazy smile of his. He had a sexy mouth, she decided, even more so when that dimple of his suddenly slipped out and made an appearance.

Thank God she was sitting down because she actually felt a little weak-kneed at the moment. Then she realized she was no better than three-quarters of the women in this city and deliberately turned her head.

Okay, Jack *more* than looked the part. More importantly, Jack looked good enough to make her fiancé jealous—which was all she wanted him to do. Of course, there was a remote possibility a man like Jack would already have plans for tonight, but that was just too darn bad.

She was his fake girlfriend. And they had a deal.

Chapter Five

As Sabrina and Jack walked into the restaurant, she smoothed the front of her black-and-white dress. It was a little skimpy for this time of year, but she'd forgo the warmth for the added attention she hoped to get from David. Casually flipping her hair from her shoulder, she scanned the room. Since it was Tuesday, only three-quarters of the tables were filled, making the job a little easier.

The Ram's Horn sat along the Massachusetts Bay coast about two towns over from her apartment. The inside of the restaurant was decorated in a traditional decor of Chippendale furniture and brass chandeliers. A wood-burning fireplace and soft candlelight enhanced the formal, open-spaced dining room. Not only was it voted "Most Romantic Dining" by *Boston* magazine, but the food was exquisite.

They were shown to a nice table overlooking the bay, and giving one last glance around, she sat down next to Jack. "I don't see David," she whispered, picking up her menu.

Jack straightened his tie and glanced at his watch. "Maybe we should have a drink before we order dinner then. It could be a while before he shows up."

"Oh, I don't drink on weekdays. Only Fridays and Saturdays."

He rolled his eyes. "You even have a schedule for *that*?"

"No," she said defensively. "Not really. I just don't like to drink on weeknights, because alcohol affects me more than it does most people."

"Oh, yeah?"

She caught the ominous gleam in his eye and waved a finger at him. "Don't get any funny ideas. We're here on a mission."

"True. But I think this *mission* would be more enjoyable for both of us if you could just relax."

Her palms were wet and her blood pressure was closely approaching stroke range, but she still shook her head. "Oh, no," she insisted. "I don't want my head all fuzzy. I want to be in total control of what I say when David gets here. Everything has to be perfect for this to be believable."

He shrugged. "You're the boss." He picked up his menu and after a moment, lowered it again. "Do you eat here a lot? And if the answer is yes, my father is paying you way too much."

She let out a chuckle. "No. David and I would come here on special occasions though. This is where he proposed to me."

Jack cocked his head and regarded her thoughtfully. "So, how did you and Dr. Wonderful meet, anyway?"

She folded her hands and smiled to herself, remembering as though it were yesterday. "I had ordered a pizza one night, and when it was delivered, I didn't have enough money. That in itself is very unusual because I always go to the ATM on Thursdays."

"Of course you do," he muttered.

She frowned. "Do you want to hear the story or not?"

"Oh, I'm sure the best part is coming up, so please continue."

She smiled tightly. "Thank you. Anyway, as luck would have it, David happened to be walking by my door at that exact moment, and he gallantly stopped and paid the delivery boy for me. I invited him in to share it with me after that, and we ended up talking all night. And the rest, I guess, is history," she said with a light laugh.

Jack stared at her over his menu. The smile that had been hanging on his lips slowly faded. "Is that it?" he asked.

"For your information, it was very romantic."

"Yep," he said, amusement lighting his eyes. "They don't write romances like that anymore."

"Excuse me, Mr. Playboy-of-the-Month, but David was sweet and generous. Traits that are hard to find in *some* people."

"Oh, I don't know." He leaned in as the corners of his mouth lifted. "Take out the office mishaps we've had, and you might think I was pretty sweet and generous, too."

"I doubt that. You wouldn't know a thing about putting someone other than yourself first. Not even your own father."

He frowned. "My own father?"

"Yes. I mean, really, Jack, how could you?"

Jack looked stunned at her outburst, but she couldn't help herself. All the feelings she had pent up over how callously he treated his family brewed to the surface and bubbled over. "Family should be the most important thing in your life. It would be to me. When your dad was in the hospital last month, he needed you. I know because I was there and visited him. And where were you? In Los Angeles with your latest TMZ headliner. You should have been there for him. It was despicable for you not to come home."

Jack's blue eyes turned to ice, and for a second she almost became fearful of the change in them.

"*You*," he said carefully and slowly as if he was using every ounce of control he had not to lunge across the table at her, "know nothing about my family or my relationship with my father—or *me*, for that matter. You're right that family is important, and you're also right that I should have been there. But you don't know any of the circumstances that kept me away, so don't for one second try to pretend you do."

She stilled. "Circumstances?"

"Yes," he said between clenched teeth. "I don't know why I even feel the need to explain myself, but I can see that if I don't, these issues are only going to sprout up again, so we might as well clear the air. Yes, I took some time off and went to California to see my girlfriend, who was participating in her first runway event for charity. It was important to her I be there. In fact, so important, she erased the messages I'd received about my father's hospitalization. She didn't think it was serious enough for me to leave, but—unlike you—knew I would. It wasn't until my dad was about to be released that my sister managed to get ahold of me."

"Oh." The heat on her cheeks sprung up as fast as a slap in the face. She dropped her chin to her chest and mumbled, "I didn't know that."

"Obviously."

"I'm sorry, Jack."

He pinched the bridge of his nose and sighed. "Whatever."

"No, really, I am. I had no right to judge you like that."

"It goes with the territory. The stockholders probably thought the same thing. Why should you be any different?"

She bit her lip. No, she wasn't any different from them or anyone else, but the fact that Jack thought that about her made her feel small. "I'll make it up to you."

"You don't have to. However, if you insist, I think I might like where this is going," he said with a small grin.

She squelched a laugh, relieved that the tension between them had lifted. "I meant, I'll do my best to help change public opinion of you."

Something in those blue eyes of his shifted as his gaze captured hers. "Actually, I hadn't expected anything less than the very best from you."

Her cheeks heated, feeling unexpectedly touched by his words. "Thanks."

"You really are loyal to my dad, aren't you?"

"Yes, I am." She didn't hesitate in answering.

"Even though he passed you over for a senior position?"

"Well, I was a little surprised at first, but the more I thought about it, the more I realized I can't fault him for preferring his own son over me." As much as she admired and respected the man, she knew blood was thicker than water. But it still hurt because he'd been like a father figure to her up until that point.

Jack sat back, his eyebrows lifting. "Ah. I took the job you wanted. And here lies the real reason for the animosity you have toward me."

"Perhaps. Although your personality might have a little to do with it," she said, hiding a smile. "On the other hand, your father has always treated me kindly, almost like a daughter."

Jack's brows creased together in a dark V as he took a large bite of a roll and chewed. "I know my dad is great—there's no denying that—but what about your own father?"

She pensively ran a hand through her hair and glanced over her shoulder. She hated answering questions about her parents. Even after all these years, the wound still stung deep. No one could understand how much it hurt to lose them so suddenly and find herself so alone. She certainly didn't want to share that information or anything else about herself with Jack. It was too personal, and she wanted to keep things between them as businesslike as she could. Thankfully, she was saved from answering when she saw David and the redhead enter the restaurant.

Her head spun back around. "He's here," she said eagerly.

Jack peered over her head and frowned. "Huh, your fiancé sure has some taste in women. First you, now her. Yet for some reason, *I'm* the one who always gets demonized. If that's not media bias, I don't know what is."

She looked at him incredulously. "Once again it's all about you. Are you this way all the time, or is this strictly for my benefit?"

He chuckled. "I aim to please."

"Well, aim it elsewhere. You're not helping matters."

"Okay, calm down and act as if you're enjoying my witty banter," he said, looking back out into the dining room.

"They're walking this way."

"Oh, gosh," she moaned. She wasn't sure she could confront David. She was such a wimp. What was she going to say? She'd have to play it light and breezy. Pretend it was a total coincidence she and Jack ended up at the same restaurant on the same night.

She took a deep breath. It was time to put up or shut up if she wanted him back. With all the muscle force in her face, she summoned up what she hoped was her most captivating smile—then said a quick prayer she didn't have lipstick on her teeth.

"Save it," Jack told her. "They're walking the other way now."

Her face immediately fell, and she let out a huge rush of air. "Where are they? I'm afraid to look."

"They're sitting diagonally from us, across the room."

"Can they see us?"

He looked at her. "I can see them, can't I?"

"You know what I mean."

He peered back up and nodded. "Your doctor can see us if he decides to look left."

Their waiter approached, and they gave their orders. Jack ordered the filet mignon and she decided on the spinach quiche. Her stomach was in knots. She was sure she wouldn't be able to eat a crumb, but she didn't want it to appear as though she and Jack were there for any other reason than dinner.

After the waiter walked away, Jack lifted his chair and slid closer to her. "We better look cozy," he explained, when she slanted him a look.

She remained silent and took a sip of ice water to calm

her nerves. This was a mistake. She felt so pathetic. Why had she let Jack talk her into this whole scheme in the first place?

What would her parents think about her sitting in a lovely romantic restaurant attempting to make her ex-fiancé jealous? Not only that, but with a man who was practically a stranger.

She should accept her fate the way it was dealt, cancel her dinner order, and leave with her dignity still intact. With the kind of luck she'd been having, David wouldn't even know she was there anyway.

Resigned to throw in the towel and finally act like an adult, she turned to inform Jack she'd changed her mind. But before she could get the beginning of a syllable out, he wrapped his arms around her and pulled her in close. She panicked, half afraid and half excited he was about to kiss her, and shoved him away. Hard.

"What is your problem?" Jack asked, rubbing where her fist slammed into his chest. "You want David to be jealous. *Remember*?"

"M-making out in a public place is not what I had in mind," she said, in a voice several octaves higher than she'd intended.

Breathe, Sabrina. She held a hand to her forehead and tried to regain some composure. It wound her up more than it should have to be held in Jack's arms. Obviously, she hadn't thought this thing all the way through. She'd told him she didn't want to kiss him, but she hadn't counted on having any real contact with Jack either—or him smelling so incredible.

"Sheesh, I had no idea I was fake dating such a prude."

She slapped her hand on the table. "I am *not* a prude."

Jack held up his hands. "Hey, take it easy now. I'm just saying that it would have been nice to know ahead of time. I'm not knocking it, if that's how you are. After all, different strokes for different folks."

The way Jack's eyebrows lifted in challenge told her he was deliberately baiting her, but she couldn't let it go. Her anxiety was through the roof and now mixed with her temper, it made for a bad combination.

Without hesitation, she grabbed him by his Herculean shoulders and pulled him in. "How's this for different strokes," she fumed, then planted her mouth directly on top of his.

Ha! She had taken him by surprise, all right. His jaw tensed and his arms froze at his sides. She'd show him who the prude was in this fake relationship. She pressed harder, parted her lips, and gave him everything she had.

It didn't take more than a second for Jack to respond. He brought his hands up to the sides of her face, holding her steady as he took control of the kiss. There was a dreamy intimacy between their mouths now. His tongue touched hers, then moved, sliding slowly and easily inside her mouth. Seconds went by and— *Oh. My.* The man could kiss. She had been prepared for that, but not how surprisingly gentle his lips were. She was powerless to resist, and with a small sigh, she settled further into them.

This is crazy. She was crazy—and in way further over her head than she'd realized. She clung to him, kissing him back, wanting him. Her instinctive response to him was overwhelming. Once again Jack surprised her. For a man who seemed to pride himself on no-nonsense actions in business, he sure took his time when it came to exploring a woman's mouth. Blindly, her lips continued to follow his, and all thoughts of who she was kissing and even why flew out the window. She couldn't remember David kissing her with this much passion. Now, she could barely remember her own name.

Until she heard it called a short distance away. "Sabrina?"

Her sanity returned, and she pulled away from Jack. Struggling to regain her breath, she closed her eyes, but not before she caught the troubled expression tattooed on Jack's face.

Well. Good.

"*Sabrina*," the voice said again.

She blinked up. David stood a foot in front of her. The sight of his annoyed face quickly cut through Jack's kiss-induced haze and brought her mind back to clear working order.

Oh no. *How long has David been standing there?*

Blood pounded in her temples. She tried to look pleasantly surprised, but she would have settled for just plain pleasant. Her feelings were bouncing all over the place, and she forgot how she was supposed to act.

David's gaze swung to Jack, eyeing him up and down as he spoke. "I've been trying to get your attention, Sabrina. I saw you and wanted to come over and say hello. Obviously, your attention was elsewhere."

Sabrina observed David with interest. He carefully straightened his already perfect tie and twice ran a hand through his fine blond hair. Both things she knew he did when his temper was stirred. However, she didn't know if she should be doing cartwheels about that or calling it a night.

She licked her lips and involuntarily shivered when she still tasted Jack. "I—"

"Yes, she was occupied," Jack interrupted. He threw an arm around her as if to drive his point home and gave her shoulder a gentle squeeze.

She swallowed hard. "Uh, David," she began again carefully, "this is…this is…"

What was wrong with her brain?

Jack stuck out a large hand. "Jack Brenner."

David seemed reluctant but eventually shook his hand. "Brenner?" His already marked frown went farther downhill. "Are you related to the Brenner of Brenner Capital, where Sabrina works?"

"Yes, that's my father."

David gave Jack a long, inscrutable look, then turned his back to give Sabrina his full attention. "Darling, may I have a word with you for a moment?"

She blinked. *Darling?*

Sabrina wished she had ordered a drink now. David was out with another woman, she had kissed another man, yet she was still "Darling"? She didn't know what was going on anymore.

"Um, of course." She pushed back from the table and stood, her legs still feeling like rubber after that kiss. "I'll be right back," she told Jack.

Jack reached for her hand. "Don't be long. I want to pick up right where we left off when you come back," he said, holding her wrist against his warm lips for an exaggerated length of time.

Her lips felt swollen, and as she remembered the underlying passion of their impromptu kiss, her cheeks ignited.

She tugged her hand away and shot him a warning look in return. What was Jack doing? He was laying it on way too thick. And worse, she was halfway to believing it.

David seemed oblivious to her and Jack's silent argument. Thank goodness. She slipped her arm through his and let him lead her out of the dining room, feeling more than a little relieved to get away from Jack and his all-too-consuming lips. She needed this time away from him to refocus on their plan and what they were doing. Because as much as she knew that kiss between her and Jack was nothing more than anger and wrongly channeled fake emotions, a small part of it had begun to feel real.

And that was something she definitely couldn't let happen again.

Chapter Six

Sabrina followed David into the dimly lit bar and pulled out a soft leather stool to sit down. He remained standing, holding a meditative look across his boyishly handsome face. She shifted uncomfortably. She felt like one of his patients, and the prognosis looked bad.

It probably gave David the shock of his life to see her out with another man. Hands fisted in her lap, she decided to wait him out and let him speak first. For once since their breakup, she had some advantage. He was the one out with another woman and all she did was...turn a simple dinner out with a man she barely knew into a bad soap-opera audition.

Oh, Lord. What on earth had possessed her to kiss Jack like that? Her own eager response shocked her. She didn't want to think about how warm and sweet his lips felt against hers or the way Jack seemed to savor each and every moment of it as much as she had.

No. It was all wrong. She was just…lonely and Jack had just…been there. That feeling was a minor blip on her radar and nothing more.

Sabrina took a deep breath and met David's gaze. David was who she wanted, who she was in love with. *Don't blow this*, she reminded herself.

"So that was the infamous Jack?" he finally said. "Your *friend* from the office?"

She swallowed. "Yes, but —"

"I had no idea you meant Jack Brenner when you mentioned you were getting advice from a Jack at work. Wow, this is obviously all my fault."

"I— Wait." She stared at him closely. "What's all your fault?"

"You out at dinner with him tonight. You're the perfect pickings for a womanizer like that."

"I am?"

"Of course you are. We've separated, and now he's suddenly pretending to be your friend. You look beautiful tonight, by the way. No wonder that guy had his hands all over you."

She blinked in astonishment. She couldn't remember the last time David paid her a compliment like that. That had to be a good sign. Although, it didn't thrill her like it should have.

David began pacing the small corner of the bar. "However, I was talking to Rose about it before I came over to your table, so I feel good about this." He nodded more to himself. "Yes, it'll be okay now."

What? No punch in the gut could have been delivered with more accuracy. She looked down at her hands folded tightly in her lap and sighed. So much for holding out for hope and good signs. David couldn't care less. No, that wasn't true—he actually seemed pleased she was lip-locked with another man. What a fool she was.

"It's fine because I'm glad I saw it and can warn you," he added. "Thank God he's not your type or else I'd be worried."

Her head snapped up. "Wait. But you should be worried. Uh, *very* worried. Didn't you see the way Jack kissed me? He wants to be more than friends."

He stopped pacing and raised his brows at her. "I'm sure he does. But don't be lulled into his web, Sabrina. I know I'm the last person who should be saying this, but he can't give you any kind of commitment. I've read articles about him. Sure, he's good-looking," he confirmed, waving his hand around dismissively, "and it's probably flattering to have his attention, but it won't last."

She didn't know why, but she felt strangely compelled to defend Jack for more reasons than their plan to make David jealous. "Jack's a different person. All those women are in the past. He's looking to settle down."

David scoffed. "That's not what I've read. Stop seeing him."

"No, I won't." A thick blanket of outrage settled over her. "I'm obviously not looking for a relationship, but I see no harm in continuing my friendship with him, since Jack and I are partners now at work."

He reached out and took hold of her shoulders in a firm grip. "Work is one thing. But as your fiancé, I have a say in who you should be hanging out with outside of work."

She swatted his hands away. "You're out with another

$\mathcal{F}$ IANCÉ $\mathcal{B}$ Y $\mathcal{F}$ ATE

woman. Don't I have any say in that?"

"Rose is just a friend, so technically, that's different."

She folded her arms, afraid she would swat him again. "Well, *technically*, I'm not your fiancée."

"You don't mean that. You're not acting like yourself. Can't you see he's using you? That man does not look like he's done sowing his wild oats, if you know what I mean."

Wild oats? Ha! *What century are we in?*

She stood. "David, I can see if we keep talking about this we're only going to cause a scene. I appreciate the warning, but until we're officially back together—*if* we get back together—I'm going to be friends with whomever I choose. I can take care of myself."

"Fine. I guess if you feel the need to see someone else to be sure of our relationship, then I'll have to deal with that. However, for your protection and because I care, I'm going to keep my eye on him." He marched back into the dining room, his jaw set with resolve.

Sabrina turned and asked the bartender for a glass of ice. When he handed it to her she took out a cube and ran it over her warm cheeks. She wasn't used to having heated discussions like that with David. But he did have a habit of telling her what to do—something she'd overlooked in the past, but now it only annoyed her.

She couldn't believe David actually threatened to keep an eye on Jack. She'd like to know how he was going to do that with the hours he kept at the hospital. And she could pick her own friends, thank you very much. Of all the high-handed things he'd ever said to her. It was as if he turned into one of those stereotypical jealous boyfriends. Who knows what possessed him to—

Wait a minute, wait a minute, wait just a darn minute... Giddiness rushed over her. David was acting *jealous*. He was actually jealous of her relationship with Jack.

She wanted to jump up and high-five the closest person around, but glancing around the sedate room, she gave up on that idea and settled on just knowing that Jack's plan had worked. So far.

She had to give Jack credit, though she still felt funny about lying to David. But once they were back together and she told David the truth, they'd probably have a huge laugh over it. It'd be a story to tell their grandkids someday.

The piano player in the corner of the bar sat down and began to play "Chances Are." She considered that another good sign. If she hadn't left her purse at the table with Jack, she would have tipped the man generously. He managed to hit it right on the nose with the perfect song.

Chances of her and David getting back together were looking better and better.

When Sabrina returned to the table, she quickly noted that Jack wore the same aggravated expression she'd just seen on David.

"*That* was the infamous David?" he charged at her before she could even sit down. "He seemed pretty ordinary to me. From the way you were talking, I half expected him to turn something he touched into gold."

She sat down, too happy with how things worked out with David to be affected by Jack's grumpy attitude. "Well, I know he's not some god."

"You can say that again. And did you see what your boy did? He didn't even want to shake my hand until I pressed him."

"Can you blame him? His fiancée is out at dinner with another man. Not only that, but we probably looked like Siamese twins joined at the lips."

"*Ex*-fiancée," he corrected. Her comment seemed to take the wind out of his anger. "And that kiss was nothing," he murmured.

Sabrina stiffened. Nothing? If she had been wearing socks, they would've been effectively and unequivocally knocked off. But of course it was meaningless to someone like him. Jack had much more experience and probably tossed around those types of kisses like confetti on New Year's Eve. She couldn't let herself forget that.

"What did he want?" he asked.

"For your information, our plan is working."

His brows rose almost imperceptibly. "Is it?"

"Yes, so thank you." By the look on his face, she could tell Jack was surprised. Maybe even a little worried. She wondered if he thought she'd renege on their deal now.

"So, what? Are you guys back together now?"

"Not exactly." She paused and glanced behind her to where David was eating with the other woman. He sat unsmiling and his face looked flustered. "David did say some things that look very promising, though."

"I'll be the judge of that," Jack said, sitting back with folded arms. "What did he say? And don't leave anything out."

"For one thing he warned me not to see you anymore. Let's see, what else— Oh, and he said, and I quote, 'That man does not look like he's done sowing his wild oats.'"

Jack's eyes narrowed. "Is that right?"

"Mm-hmm." She grinned, enjoying Jack's reaction, but not exactly certain why. "He wants to protect me and said he'll be watching you closely."

"That's it." He tossed his napkin on the table and stood. "Dr. Too Good's going down."

"No!" She grabbed hold of his hand. "No, don't. Sit down. Can't you see that's good?" She tugged on his arm again. "It means he's concerned."

Jack stared into her eyes for a full five seconds, the anger working in his cheeks, then grudgingly sat back down. "What is there to be so concerned about? I'm not Charles Manson here. I'm a very decent guy. I've never even had so much as a parking ticket in my life."

"That's not the point. He thinks you're some playboy and that you'll break my heart." She let out a rush of air when Jack seemed to settle down. That's all she needed was him getting into a fistfight over a little name-calling. Why would he even care what David said anyway? They weren't dating for real.

But after a moment, she couldn't help but ask, "So is David right?"

"About what?"

"Are you still sowing your wild oats?"

"Hmm, I'm not sure," he said, scratching his chin. "I'd have to get my time machine and travel back to when that phrase was used to fully understand the question."

She rolled her eyes, but chuckled. "Well, are you looking for a special kind of woman?"

His dimple slipped out. "Of course."

"That special woman to share the rest of your life and

possibly have children with?" she finished.

"Hell no."

She raised an eyebrow. "Then I guess David's right."

"The good doctor knows nothing about me or my oats. At least I have the decency to be up front with a woman and not leave her dangling while I make up my mind. She knows exactly what's she's getting into with me. Light and fun, no strings attached."

"Why don't you want to get married?"

Jack looked taken aback by her question. "I already feel married. To my job. As far as I'm concerned, it's been the best and longest relationship I've ever had."

"That's not the same. Everybody gets lonely and wants someone special in their life."

He looked away. "I'm not everybody."

No, he certainly wasn't.

She supposed it was perfectly reasonable for someone like him to *choose* to stay single for the rest of his life. A part of her even felt sorry for the choice he'd made. But she wasn't about to push the issue anymore. If Jack wanted to spend the rest of his life meeting strange woman after strange woman, she wasn't going to lose any sleep over it. And if he wanted to end up living and dying alone in some old-age home in Florida, she certainly wasn't going to give it a second thought.

Except she did. And it bothered her that she did.

The waiter came and interrupted their fallen silence with their entrees. Although Jack's steak looked and smelled delicious, she shook her head at it. "I've noticed you eat a lot of red meat."

"Careful," he chided with a grin. "First you talk marriage

and now you're telling me what to eat. You're sounding more and more like a real girlfriend every day. Just remember, this is still our first date, so keep your hands to yourself tonight. I'm not one of *those* guys."

"Jack, I'm serious. Your dad's been battling heart issues and that kind of thing is hereditary."

He stabbed a piece of steak with his fork and pointed it at her. "Has David ever mentioned anything to you about your bossiness?"

"Never," she said, suppressing a smile. "And I'm not saying you have to become a vegetarian. But eating like one for even one day a week reduces consumption of saturated fat by fifteen percent, enough to ward off lifestyle diseases such as heart attacks, strokes, and cancer, too."

"Suggestion noted, *darling*," he mumbled around a mouthful of meat.

"See?" She chuckled. "You're sounding more and more like a real boyfriend, too."

"How about we celebrate our successes, then," he suggested. "Perhaps you could bend your rule just this once and have a little champagne with me."

"Well…" She bit her lip. She supposed she could splurge a little, considering. "Okay. Why not?"

At once, Jack signaled the waiter and asked for the wine list. After spending a total of three seconds looking it over, he ordered what she hoped was a reasonably priced bottle of champagne.

After the waiter came back and poured them both a healthy glass, Sabrina reached for hers but ended up knocking over the table salt. She gasped. Quickly gathering up what spilled on the table, she threw it over her shoulder.

Jack frowned over his glass. "Good grief, what was that?"

"Hmm?" Feeling more at ease, she took a tentative sip of her wine. She was a bit of a wine novice, but she thought the champagne tasted crisp and delicious.

"The whole salt ritual you just performed. What was that all about?"

"Oh." Her cheeks heated. "Spilling salt is bad luck. But if you throw it over your left shoulder with your right hand, then it's supposed to counteract it with good luck."

"I heard something different." He signaled with his index finger to lean closer and lowered his voice. "Do you want to know what it really means?"

"Sure, what?"

"It means you now have salt on your shoulder."

She picked up her fork and made a face. "Well, that's not what I've read."

"Superstitious?" There was a glint of amusement in the depths of his blue eyes.

"A little," she murmured. Oh, who was she kidding? The way her luck was working, if she had time to stop off and buy a lottery ticket tonight, she probably would.

"How about a toast?" He lifted his flute.

"Okay," she said, mimicking his gesture. "To successful goals?"

They clinked glasses, then Jack drank deeply, finishing off his glass. She did the same. Her head was already feeling a bit dizzy. Maybe champagne was a bad idea. Or maybe she was caught up in the excitement of tonight—that kiss, her fight with David, Jack's odd behavior.

Jack was definitely different tonight. He wasn't supposed to be charming or funny. He should be annoying and self-righteous. She thought she'd be counting down the seconds until her "date" with him was over. But instead, she found she was enjoying herself. Jack had a way of sneaking up on her, like a cold or…a chin hair. She had to turn away from that easygoing smile of his to even remember what they'd toasted to.

Successful goals, stupid. David, *not* Jack's ocean-blue eyes.

"Is David looking over here?" she asking, forcing herself to concentrate on what mattered.

"Nope."

"He's not?" She was so sure David would be seething and unable to keep his eyes off them. What happened in the span of ten minutes?

"Wait, he just looked over."

Aha! She knew it.

Smiling, she took a bite of her quiche and watched as Jack picked up the bottle and refilled their glasses. Now she could back to enjoying her evening with Jack. Everything was back on track. She was so happy she almost couldn't catch up with her thoughts. This was too simple, and Jack was making it way too fun. She still couldn't believe how easy it was to make David jealous. She knew all along he cared and this proved it. Soon, they'd be engaged again, just like Madame Butterfly predicted.

She sighed into her flute and took another sip. The family she always longed to have was within reach again. Her life was finally coming together. She finished off her second glass, and her mind began to float, and she felt as if she were swinging on a star. But, she wasn't worried, because no matter what, she knew from now on that star would be a lucky one.

Chapter Seven

"I promise to shut up now," Sabrina said, slapping a hand over her mouth. But she continued to talk through her palm anyway. "I've been saying way too much. That always happens when I drink champagne. And when I drink beer. Or vodka. And—"

"I get it," Jack said, entertained. "Maybe you should have a little more to eat."

She saluted. "Aye, aye." Then as she lowered her hand, it landed in her cheesecake. "Uh-oh, cleanup in aisle three."

He smothered a laugh as he tossed her his napkin. Sabrina was drunk. Well, not exactly *drunk* drunk, but she was well past her limit, which was obviously minuscule to begin with.

Not that it was his fault, Jack reminded himself again. She didn't have to finish her glass every time he refilled it for her. And whose idea was it to get a second bottle anyway?

Okay, it *was* his fault. Sabrina was going to murder

him—when she sobered up.

Too bad, because they were actually getting along for once. Now that she let her guard down, they even managed to have fun—something he hadn't had with a woman outside the bedroom in a long time.

Jack gazed across the table at her. Sabrina seemed intent on playing with her dessert and hadn't noticed him watching her. The night was chockfull of surprises. It wasn't every woman who knew just as much about baseball as he did and even enjoyed discussing it. This was the most mellow he'd seen her. Usually she was all wrapped up in anxiety and spreadsheets, which was why he couldn't resist egging her on whenever he had the chance. She made it almost too easy. And way too much fun.

There really was nothing sexier to him than a woman all riled up with anger. It was just another form of passion in his book. And Sabrina seemed to have more than an average share. Especially when she looked like she could melt an iceberg with the heat radiating from those baby-blue eyes of hers. The way her cheeks flamed pink and those soft, generous lips of hers pouted and got all—

Uh-oh. Where'd that thinking come from?

That kiss.

Mother of mercy, who knew she had such deadly precision with that mouth of hers? Something had ignited between them from the moment their lips had touched. He knew it was wrong, yet here he was wishing those lips were on his again. What an idiot he was. He couldn't involve himself with her. Hell, she barely liked him. *And* she was engaged.

Sort of.

Jack continued to study her. There was something mesmerizing about the way the candlelight reflected in her dark hair—how it flowed just slightly past her shoulders and looked smooth and glossy, like rich, melted chocolate. He was struck with an irresistible urge to reach out and feel it.

And that's when he decided to call it a night.

"All right, let's get you home," he announced.

Sabrina didn't lift her eyes from her dessert she was making fork tracks through. "What about the check?" she murmured.

"It's already paid."

She frowned. "But I told you I wanted to go Dutch."

Jack sighed. *Doesn't this woman ever turn it off?* Four sheets to the wind and she was worried about paying her share. "No, friends go Dutch. Fake girlfriends get their meals paid for by their fake boyfriends. Now let's get out of here."

Sabrina finally looked up with huge innocent eyes, the corners of her mouth sagging south. "Didn't you like your dinner?"

"Of course I liked my dinner."

"Then why are you so crabby?"

Because I can't stop thinking about those mouthwatering lips of yours and the way they moved against mine. Happy? Although, if he confessed that little nugget of truth, he doubted she'd be happy at all. "Um, you didn't offer me any of your cheesecake."

She let out a beautiful laugh. "You had your own cheesecake."

The way her smile burst through like sunshine had the direct opposite effect on his mood. "What can I say? I like to eat," he said tightly. "Come on."

"Is David still here?" she whispered.

"No, he left about twenty minutes ago."

Her fork dropped with a *clank*. "What? Did he look forlornly over here before he left?"

"I don't know," he mumbled. But the truth was David had stared at them all evening. Jack didn't know why he didn't feel like sharing that information with her. Maybe because he found David's actions rude. If Jack were dating Sabrina for real, he would have gone over there and made it known to him.

"How could you not know?" she asked. "You're supposed to be my eyes and hears."

He rolled his eyes. "You mean eyes and *ears*."

"Oh." She thought about it and nodded. "Yes, that's better."

He had to smile. "I thought so."

She glanced at her watch, and her eyes widened. "I should have called my landlord. I didn't think I'd be out this late."

"Your landlord has you on a curfew?"

She shook her head, and it flopped back and forth like a rag doll. "She's having her apartment painted, and I told her she could stay with me. She's probably asleep by now anyway."

"Well, aren't you Miss Congenial?"

She stared at him with a confused look. "No, it's Miss Cassidy," she slurred.

He couldn't help but chuckle. The woman was adorable — *too* adorable. "I need a cigarette," he murmured.

Her little nose wrinkled. "Ugh. You smoke?"

"I used to. Gave it up a few years ago, but still get the

urge when I'm stressed. Started smoking in college. Probably the least of my bad habits back then."

"Why did you start?" Sabrina rested her chin in her hand and gazed at him, all dreamy and sincere—and intoxicated. His eyes drifted to her mouth for the second time. She was doing that sexy-pout thing again.

Jack had to clear his throat. "I don't know. Probably because it got me through my mom's death a little."

She gasped. "You were so young. How did she die?"

Jack frowned. Sabrina obviously didn't realize he never talked about his mom with anyone. There were certain lines you did not cross with people unless invited. *Ever.* And she most certainly had not been issued an invitation. But as Jack continued to stare into her soft blue eyes, a small chip of his resolve was taken out.

"She committed suicide," he finally answered.

"Oh, no," she whispered in horror. "I'm sorry."

"Thanks, but you don't have to tell me that. It was a long time ago. At least it wasn't messy. She took some pills and never woke up."

"It was a long time ago, but you still must carry a part of that with you. Something like that you can't simply turn off."

Her conviction made him think she spoke from experience. But he didn't want to share any more of himself with her tonight. He preferred fun and detached—unemotional. He feverishly tried to brush off the way the warmth in her eyes was making him feel. "No, you can't turn it off, but you *can* break the nozzle."

The look on her face told him that line was an instant party killer. But he didn't want to spend time pouring his heart and soul out to her. It left him too vulnerable.

Something he hadn't been since his mother died.

"Let's go," he said shortly and stood up.

Sabrina jumped up with him, but obviously too fast, because it sent her swaying into him. Jack automatically wrapped his arms around her and stood her up straight. "Easy does it," he murmured. "Can you walk out of here?"

She nodded, then squeezing her eyes closed, shook her head.

"Okay, lean on me and we'll be home before you know it."

As they walked through the dining room together, her arms hung around his waist and she pressed herself farther into his chest. Jack gritted his teeth. Great. Couldn't she just be normal and not have to smell like some fancy vanilla dessert he could devour in one bite? What was he, made of wood? He cursed himself for that analogy, and, deciding he may have had too much to drink as well, called for a cab.

Jack led her to a plush sofa in the lobby and sat down next to her to wait for their ride. Then thinking better of it, he shifted over several inches. Then a few inches more.

Don't touch her anymore, he advised himself. *Your defenses are down, stupid. You had too much alcohol and are obviously not in your right mind.*

All he needed to do was drop her off at her place, go back home, and sleep off any effect the alcohol may have had on him tonight. Tomorrow when he woke up, she'd go back to hating him and he'd go back to thinking of her as just a nice, sweet, high-strung girl. Everything would be normal again.

After all, Jack didn't want her. He only wanted his rightful position in the company. Nothing else. Making a play for his fake girlfriend and business partner—who was practically engaged—wouldn't help his chances any.

He kept his eyes focused straight ahead and continued his mental lecture as Sabrina wiggled closer. Then on a sigh, she wove her arm through his and laid her head on his shoulder.

Jack mouthed a low curse—and wished like hell he hadn't quit smoking.

• • •

A high-pitched shriek had Sabrina's skull splitting open like a coconut.

"That's what you get for drinking on a weekday," she muttered to herself.

Spread out on her bed, she attempted to roll over but could barely move because of the pounding pain in her head. Trying to reach for the snooze button, she realized with dismay that the sound she heard hadn't come from her alarm clock.

Her head shot up when she heard another shout.

Grabbing the baseball bat hidden underneath her bed, she held her head and ran for the living room. Stopping short at the entrance of her kitchen, she saw Mrs. Metzger holding an empty glass in her hands and Jack brushing a huge red stain down the front of his white T-shirt.

"Jack!" Half out of breath, she turned to Mrs. Metzger. "What in the world's going on?"

"I'll tell you what's going on," Jack interrupted. "This woman threw tomato juice at me." Mrs. Metzger indignantly set a hand on her hip. "I could have done a lot worse. You scared the jimmies out of Theo and me."

Sabrina glanced around and saw the cat nowhere in sight. Jack's large frame, on the other hand, she'd have to be punched in both eyes to miss. No wonder Mrs. Metzger reacted the way she did. Taking up almost all the room in her tiny kitchen, Jack stood there tall and menacing with his shadowy beard and gruff expression. The look in his blue eyes practically screamed, *I'm about to blow at any second.* It almost made *her* take an involuntary step back.

However, on second glance, Jack's disheveled hair combined with the tomato dripping from his chin and chest had her biting back a laugh despite her aching head.

His angry glare now aimed in her direction. "This isn't funny."

"You're right," she agreed, struggling for composure. "Having V8 thrown in your face first thing in the morning isn't the least bit funny." She set down the bat on the counter and folded her arms at him. "But I'd like to know what you're doing here."

Jack took the stack of paper towels Mrs. Metzger handed him and began blotting his face. "You invited me to stay, but I can see I got more than I bargained for here." He cast a meaningful glance at her landlord.

Sabrina's mouth dropped open. "I did what?"

"Excuse me," Mrs. Metzger broke in. She stopped wiping the floor and inspected Jack. She seemed to like what she saw. "Who are you, anyway?"

He held out his hand, suddenly all business. "Jack Brenner. I'm the new boyfriend."

Oh, no. Sabrina gingerly held a hand over her eyes. *The lies continue…*

"Boyfriend?" Mrs. Metzger looked at Sabrina for confirmation, and she could only manage a slight shrug. "Oh, I'm very sorry," she told him, shaking his hand. "I didn't hear you two come in last night. Had I known Sabrina was going to bring home a…a guest, I wouldn't have attacked you like I did." She set down her mug and leaned slyly into Sabrina. "You did good," she said with a wink. "I'll go change now, but there's more juice in the fridge."

After Mrs. Metzger walked past them, Sabrina pinned a hard glare on Jack. "Why in the world would I ask you to stay?" she whispered heatedly.

"We both had too much to drink last night, so you told me to stay, and you'd drive me to pick up my car in the morning."

"Oh." She vaguely remembered that now, as she rubbed her forehead. It kind of made sense.

Without warning, Jack tore off his damp T-shirt in front of her, making her legs tremble a bit with anticipation of what might come off next. She stared at his bare chest, feeling even more off balance when his hands traveled to his belly button. Jack paused, then looked up at her with a hint of amusement. A rush of heat seized her cheeks, and her gaze shot to the wall behind him, then to the counter, then to the floor. She had a sneaking suspicion Jack knew his body was impressive, so she was not about to give him the satisfaction of ogling it. Yet somehow—despite her will—her eyes kept being drawn in to catch peeks of his dark chest hair. It seemed to be distributed along those sculpted pecs of his with absolute perfection.

Suddenly curious, Sabrina looked down at herself. She was still wearing the same black dress from last night. That also made sense. But something else kept nagging at her as she thought about three adults staying in her one little apartment.

She looked back up, willing her eyes on his and not his body. "Uh, Jack, where exactly did you sleep last night?"

A lazy grin swept over his rugged face. "With you."

She was afraid of that.

She lunged for the bat. "I should have known," she spat.

Jack quickly held up his hands, trying to control his laughter. "Take it easy, will you? Jeez, you're touchy. I slept with you in your room, but *on the floor*. By the way, my back's paying for that one."

"Oh." She didn't want to think about why she felt a trickle of disappointment at that. Jack had been a gentleman. That was...good. But she had to wonder if he even tried anything funny—or had wanted to. Since she was still wearing her panty hose and he complained about her bossiness last night, she guessed not.

What was the matter with her?

She wasn't interested in Jack. Why would she be? David was right. Jack wasn't even remotely her type. The man was clearly an egomaniac who probably slept with more women than there were hairs on Mrs. Metzger's cat.

"Good," she said, trying to sound pleased. "What time is it anyway?"

"Almost eight."

"Eight?" she cried. "We'll never have time to pick up your car this morning. Can you wait until after work?"

"Yeah, I'm not traveling today. You have a razor I can use?"

She nodded and held out a hand. "Let me have your

T-shirt. I'll throw it in the wash and bring it to work for you tomorrow."

He casually tossed it to her with a smile. "Thanks, *Mom*."

His comment triggered a memory of the conversation they'd had at dinner. She realized that Jack had opened up to her—their first real conversation since meeting. No wonder Jack was so anti-commitment. Having a parent commit suicide would be a lot of strain on a family. The children would have dealt with a lot of guilt issues…and worse, shattered trust.

Sabrina continued to stand there, twisting his T-shirt. "I know I had a lot to drink last night, but I did listen to everything you told me. I know it wasn't easy for you to share that."

"Not a big deal."

She licked her lips and did her best to not let his tone affect what she still wanted to say. "I know what you went through. Although my parents didn't take their own lives, someone else did. So, I know what it's like to feel lost and even question the purpose of life."

She watched his tense features slowly relax.

"I appreciate all you did for me last night," she continued, "and I thought that maybe under the circumstances, you would now consider me a friend."

"Friend?" He looked like he'd just swallowed rotten cheese, and so she safely assumed someone like Jack wasn't used to getting proposals of friendship from women.

"Yes. I think that if we were more united on a personal front, we would have a better chance of reaching our goals more quickly, don't you?"

Jack seemed to consider it over in his mind. When he

finally looked back at her, his eyes held a trace of amusement. "Okay, *friend*."

She let out a deep, pent-up breath. "Okay." About to walk back to her bedroom, she stopped midstride at the sound of Jack's voice.

"Don't forget this." He held out her baseball bat and gave her a wide, toothy grin. "I don't think you'll be needing it anymore."

"I wouldn't be too sure." She took it from his outstretched hand and winked. "We haven't been friends that long."

• • •

Sabrina finished applying her ruby lipstick, then gave her hair a quick shake. After toying around with a few strands of her bangs in front of the foyer mirror, she turned to Jack. "Okay, let's go."

"Finally," he mumbled, swinging open the front door.

"Sorry, but I don't want your father thinking I went on some drinking binge last night."

"You *did* go on a drinking binge last night. But he won't notice." His eyes swept over her with an appreciative gleam. "You look really great." When she slanted him a look, he cleared his throat. "I mean…considering."

Sabrina rolled her eyes. Men had it way too easy. Just shaving and splashing cold water on his face, Jack looked like he was ready to do another *Boston* magazine layout. Life wasn't fair that way. Although because of Mrs. Metzger, he did smell a little like a salad. She smiled in spite of herself. "Thanks, I think." She locked her door and led the way down the aisle.

"What are friends for?" he said as he fell into step beside her. "And since we're so chummy now, I think I should mention something to you."

Sabrina watched him warily. It was only thirty minutes into it and she wasn't so sure she could handle this *friends* thing with him much longer. "What's that?"

"You snore."

She stopped in the middle of the hallway and gaped. "I do not."

"Oh yeah, you do." He nodded, beaming from ear to ear. "Cute, kind of baby snores, but still snores by standard definition. Maybe that was the problem that broke up you and David. Doctors need their sleep, you know."

She shot him a withering glare. "Boy, you're kind of jolly for a man who has a sore back and took a tomato-juice shower." He chuckled as she stormed out the doors of the main entrance.

"Hey, seriously, what really caused your breakup?" Jack called after her.

Stopping at her blue Honda, she looked up. "I'm not sure." She tried to pull open her car door, but Jack pressed his hand on it, making it near impossible.

"Hold it. David didn't even give you a solid reason for breaking off the engagement?"

"Not exactly." She tried to fling his arm away, but Jack held tight.

"Why not?" he demanded. "The guy proposes, then changes his mind but gives you no real explanation. How could you let him do that to you?"

The anger in his tone had her blinking up at him. She couldn't understand why he was even pressing the issue. It was her life. Her fiancé. "David said he was confused and—" She caught sight of David's car pulling in next to them.

"Put your arms around me," she said urgently.

"Huh?"

Do I have to do everything? "It's David. Quick, do something."

In an instant, Jack pressed his hands against the car window on either side of her, pinning her in. Her head automatically fell back, and her heart started pounding so fervently through her chest, it almost hurt. She convinced herself it was because of David and what he would say, and not because of the way Jack began nuzzling her neck.

"How's that?" Jack murmured in her ear.

There was a tingling in the pit of her stomach and her mouth went bone-dry. "O...k-kay."

He smiled against her skin, sending off sensations like a domino effect throughout her entire body. She thought she would melt right into the paint of the car. And all he was using was his mouth.

Oh dear. She hated to think what her traitorous body would do if his hands were actually on her. His breath came fast and hot against her throat, but his lips were soft and caressing. If she didn't keep herself in check, she was afraid she'd almost purr.

Then he shifted closer.

His body, warm and solid, felt especially good against the freezing-cold temperature outside. It made her feel sheltered and cozy, and if she didn't know he was only acting, really...*wanted*?

No. Jack was just a better actor than she was. Telling herself she was acting too, Sabrina closed her eyes, tilting her head back to give him better access to her neckline. She could smell her own vanilla soap on his face, but somehow it didn't seem feminine at all—nothing about him could.

Her eyes sprung open when she heard David's door slam behind them, but Jack didn't immediately pull back. An itsy-bitsy part of her almost hoped he wouldn't. When Jack finally did break away, she felt a huge surge of guilt, and not being able to even glance at him, feebly turned to David. And her eyes widened. He looked awful.

"David."

"Hello," he said, his eyes only on her. "I had an emergency last night at the hospital. I'm just getting back now."

She only nodded. Little did he know, with the way he looked, he didn't have to explain.

"I'm glad I ran into you, actually," David said, taking a step closer. "I didn't have time to mention it last night, but I assume I can still count on your help with the charity dinner next Sunday?"

Her mouth almost fell open. The last thing she expected was to still be invited to attend the fund-raiser he'd been planning for months prior to their breakup. "Oh, of course. No problem." She hoped she sounded nonchalant.

David smiled warmly at her, and she found it comforting—like an old quilt. "In case I don't see you, I'll make sure I leave your ticket under your door."

"She'll need *two*, Doc," Jack added sharply.

David's smile wiped clean away as he turned to Jack with grim eyes. "Of course," he said, sounding more agreeable than he looked. "Any friend of Sabrina's is a friend of mine. See you both then." Throwing his bag over his shoulder, he stormed away.

Jack bent his head toward Sabrina but kept his eyes on David's retreating back. "Something about that guy rubs me the wrong way."

She cocked her head as she watched David walk into the building. "It seems the feeling is mutual."

"So that's your type, huh?"

"Yes, he is. Why do you ask?"

Jack shrugged. "I don't know. I guess I'm having a hard time believing someone like him is worth all that you're doing. Tell me what's so great about him."

Unfortunately, she had to think a minute. "Well, as you can see he's very dedicated to the hospital."

"Okay, you might as well say boring. You like boring."

Sabrina shoved him out of her way and opened the car door. "You're being ridiculous. I don't have to explain why I love him." She climbed in and slammed the door.

As she started the engine, Jack calmly walked around to the other side and let himself in.

The car ride remained silent for almost twenty minutes before Jack turned to her. "Stay in this lane," he told her.

Sabrina pressed her lips together and did as he said. She was expecting he'd mumble out at least one "I'm sorry" for his remark about David.

"How did your parents die?" he asked instead. His voice was different now. Low and somber. She was trying to concentrate on driving through the morning rush-hour traffic, but could feel his eyes closely set on her. It was unnerving.

"Car accident."

Jack swore under his breath.

Like the popping of a balloon, Jack's reaction deflated her anger. "At least, that's what I was told by Child Services.

I don't have any real family. Instead, I grew up in a few different foster homes until I was able to go to college and get out on my own."

Without warning, Jack laid a hand on her thigh. She tried not to stiffen at the intimate gesture, since she knew he was only trying to be comforting. And probably with any other person, it would be calming, but instead she found herself trying not to drive them off the overpass.

"So you have no family at all?" she heard Jack ask.

"No—until I met David. He was the first man to make me feel as if I wasn't alone anymore. I felt…whole. His family is wonderful, and they accepted me as a part of it so quickly. It was weird, meeting him the way I did, and then getting engaged. Everything about it was just so perfect. It was like fate," she added. "I guess you can see now why I would want him back so badly."

"No."

Hands tight on the wheel, Sabrina glanced over at him.

He was serious.

"You don't?" Frowning hard, she made a quick left and pulled into the parking garage only a block from their building.

"No," he repeated, finally removing his hand from her leg. "Do you really think he's so great just because of his family?"

"Well." She cleared her throat, not sure if she should share her superstitions with him. "No. Like I said, there are other reasons—"

"Yeah well, what I'm not hearing is that he *does it* for you."

"He *does it* for me." It sounded like more of a question,

even to her own ears. She hoped Jack hadn't picked up on it.

"Wow, convincing."

She winced. He had picked up on it. She fisted her hands tightly around the steering wheel. "Look, I don't have to convince you of anything. David is what I want and that's that."

"Sabrina, do you really think David—love—is worth everything you're going through?"

"Of course it is."

Jack snorted. "I don't think so. Putting everything you have into one person is a setup for an emotional disaster. At least your parents went together. I saw what the death of my mom did to my dad. It wasn't pretty."

After turning off the motor, she turned and gave him a solid look. "Just because you've seen a bad side to love and marriage doesn't mean there aren't any good sides to it."

Jack checked his watch. "We'd better get going."

She nodded and then stepped out of the car. It was obvious talk of marriage and love made Jack uncomfortable. And just as she hoped he respected her beliefs, she would have to respect his.

Jack walked around the car, and when he did, he stopped, contemplating her. "How can you be so sure this thing with David will really last?"

"I'm not. But I'll never know unless I try. I think if you ever found the right woman, you'd understand what I was talking about."

He met her gaze for a long moment. "Yeah, maybe," he said, finally turning and walking away.

But he didn't sound swayed.

Chapter Eight

Friday afternoon, Jack wearily walked onto the elevator and pushed thirty-two. He'd been traveling all week but was finally able to schedule an in-office day and catch up on some paperwork. He hoped to catch up with Sabrina as well. They'd both been so busy, they'd only managed to communicate by leaving each other voice mails. Voice mails, he noted sourly, that were business-related only. After all that talk she gave him last week about friendship, he assumed she'd mention if anything had progressed with her fiancé. But she hadn't said a thing about David.

Interesting.

Sabrina didn't belong with someone like David—not that he was an expert on love. But Jack had been there in the parking lot last week, saw how they interacted. The reserved politeness between them had him shaking his head. She deserved much better. Someone who could appreciate her loyalty and quick wit.

Her *sexiness*.

That thought suddenly had his teeth aching. But it was the truth. He was actually enjoying this pretend-boyfriend stuff with her. Maybe a little too much. How could he not when she smelled sweeter than honey and fit so perfectly in a man's arms? Unfortunately, Jack was not looking for the kind of relationship Sabrina wanted. *Marriage. Commitment.*

His insides shuddered.

No, she deserved better than Jack, too. Plus, she was counting on him to help her.

And help he did. When Sabrina had demanded he do something while David was watching, he had actually ended up doing the *second* thing that popped into his mind. Ninety-nine percent certain he would have been slapped for the first, he was glad at the time for his decision. Although with the way she'd reacted, he now wondered.

Against her car, he had felt her body humming to *his* touch — and not her precious doctor's. The way her breathing had almost stopped, her pulse scrambling under his lips. It was irresistible. Sabrina could protest all she wanted that she was in love with David, but she couldn't hide the fact that she *wanted* Jack.

And he wanted her.

There. He admitted it. There was no alcohol in his system this time.

He wanted her. Big deal. He'd wanted lots of women in his lifetime. And even some women he knew he couldn't have. In fact, he had just been fantasizing about Scarlett Johansson last month, but he wasn't knocking on *her* door.

It wasn't like he couldn't rein in his hormones. After all,

he had no right interfering with Sabrina's engagement. And he wouldn't—if that's what she truly wanted.

The elevator doors finally opened. As soon as Jack walked onto the main floor, he searched out Sabrina. He frowned when he noticed she wasn't at her desk.

"Oh, hey, Jack," Christine Young said, stopping in front of him. "I bet it's nice not to be on the road for a change, huh?"

Jack glanced over Chris's blond head and still didn't see Sabrina anywhere. "Yeah, it's great, but I still have a lot of work to do," he said, his gaze roaming the room. "Have you seen Sabrina?"

"She's in the lounge area right now, trying to get some quiet."

Jack's gaze snapped to Chris. "She's sick?"

Chris nodded. "Bad headache. She gets them every now and then. She's out of pain reliever, so I was just about to run down to the store for her."

"I'll take care of it."

"You don't have to do that. I'm sure—"

"I said I'll take care of it."

Chris blinked at him. He hadn't meant for his words to come out so gruffly, but Sabrina was his responsibility. Because…they were partners. And friends. "Sorry," he said with a sheepish smile. "I know where I can get something close by, that's all."

Chris hesitated but then smiled back. "Um, okay, that would be great."

He turned around and headed back toward the elevators, his pulse racing. Sabrina never mentioned anything about headaches. She should have told him. Was she getting headaches because of work stress? She was naturally high-strung, but he hoped he hadn't put any added pressure on her. Maybe he'd talk to her about it.

"Jack," Chris called out.

Half distracted by his thoughts about Sabrina's workload, he glanced behind him. "What?"

"Are you feeling all right?"

He stopped and punched the elevator. When it didn't open right away, he eyed the stairs. "I'm feeling fine. Why?" he snapped, pressing the elevator button again.

She shook her head in bewilderment. "Um, no reason, I guess."

When Jack returned to the office, he headed straight for the lounge. Sitting there at the table, Sabrina was hunched over with her head held in her hands. He wasn't a doctor, like her precious David, but she didn't look good.

Standing over her in two strides, he gently placed a hand on her back. "Hey, how are you feeling?"

She didn't move, and for a moment, he thought he spoke too quietly for her to hear. "Don't yell," she whispered. "My head is killing me. It feels like a migraine coming on."

"Did you take anything yet?"

"No," she groaned. "Nobody has anything. I asked Chris to run out to the store for me."

"You didn't ask *me*." He tried to keep his tone light, even a little consoling, but, man, he was frustrated. The woman was obviously hurting. She knew he'd be coming into the office today. You'd think she would have asked *him* for help.

She slowly pulled her hands away and squinted up at him. "You carry pain reliever?"

Her face was pale, and her pupils large as dinner plates. She seemed so fragile, like a wounded child. He hated seeing her like this. "No, but here." He slapped three bottles on the table and went to get some water.

Sabrina looked at the various OTC medicines in amazement. "Wow, I had no idea you were a walking pharmacy," she said, picking up the ibuprofen.

He pushed a Dixie cup of water into her hands and shrugged. "I'm not. You just have to know where to ask. Here." He handed her a wrapped doughnut, too. "Maybe you should eat something."

She glanced at the doughnut, then to the ibuprofen bottle, and then back up at Jack again. "Where did you get all this?"

"What's with all the questions? Hurry up and take it. You're in pain, remember?"

He hadn't meant to raise his voice. Yeah, maybe he was overreacting, but the expression she had on her face was making him feel like some sort of superhero. And he was far from that. He just didn't want her to be in pain.

Her eyes turned wary, but she ended up swallowing the tablets. "Thanks, Jack." She drank some more water, then smiled up at him gratefully. "You are a good friend. I owe you."

Jack's heart almost bottomed out. That smile. It killed him every time.

Sabrina had a great smile. Actually, she had an incredible smile. And he'd seen it plenty of times these last couple of weeks. But this one was different. It was all for him. That alone was payment enough. Almost.

Almost? What was going on with him?

Her smile faltered. "You don't look so good yourself. Are you feeling okay?"

He mentally shook himself. "I'm fine," he bit out. "I have a lot of work to do. Trying to help my dad, too. He's noticed a slight drop in performance—present company excluded—in the associate wholesalers. I'm trying to come up with a plan. I'm hoping to show the board I'm more than just a pretty face around here."

She cracked a smile, pointing the doughnut at him. "You didn't ask *me*," she said wryly.

He raised an eyebrow. "You have a plan?"

"Maybe. If you really want to look good to the board, you could work out some kind of bonus system based on how much they help in acquiring sales."

"We couldn't afford it. That would mean we'd have to take the money out of the senior wholesaler commission. I'm not sure they'd go for the pay cut."

"With the kind of salary those wholesalers are making, I doubt it would make much of a difference. Besides, it doesn't necessarily have to translate to a drop in their salary. If the internal assistant boosts sales because of the incentive, it would mean more money for both."

Jack considered her idea and had to admit it wasn't half-bad. "I'll think about it. Thanks for your help."

"Just trying to show you I'm more than a pretty face, too."

Jack smiled, but he already knew Sabrina was smart and a good problem-solver. But because of their past animosities, he'd never told her. Not that she would have believed him anyway.

Sabrina suddenly got a funny look on her face, and her hand shot to her head. "What's the matter?" he asked.

"Nothing," she said rubbing the back of her neck. "It just feels like the pain is shooting up from my shoulders now. I guess I've been sitting hunched over too long."

"I can help with that." He cracked his knuckles. "Allow me to perform the *Jack Brenner special*," he said, wiggling his fingers in front of her.

"Which is?"

"A shoulder massage."

Her back went poker straight. "Oh, uh…no thanks… uh…I don't think…"

He chuckled, finding her reaction to being touched by him particularly interesting. "I'm hardly going to take advantage of you in broad daylight in the middle of work. Unless you want me to, of course."

"I don't."

"Then you're just going to have to trust me."

She gave him a long, guarded look, then finally nodded. "Well, okay."

"Aww, you do trust me. I'm touched. Trust is such an important quality to have in a fake relationship." He shifted behind her and placed his hands on her shoulders. "Now just unbutton your shirt."

She jerked a hand to her throat. *"What?"*

"Easy, I don't know what's on *your* mind," he said, grinning, "but this is strictly professional on my end." Her expression didn't show great confidence in his words, so he stuck out his bottom lip and tried to look as sincere as possible. "Two buttons—maybe three—that's all I ask. I need access to those shoulder muscles."

Sabrina hesitated for several seconds. "There," she said, unbuttoning one, then sending him a sharp look. "That should be plenty of *access*."

"Fine, now let your mind drift." His hands began working her shoulders. Man, she was tense. Her muscles were like cement, and they were hardening the more he touched them. No wonder she was prone to stress headaches. Sabrina probably slept anxious.

"Will you relax?" he scolded lightly. "You're going to sprain my hands, and I'll have to eat with my feet."

She let out a chuckle, and her shoulders softened. "Sorry," she murmured.

Smiling to himself, he leisurely ran his thumbs over the contours of her delicate neck muscles as his fingers began to knead and press. Once he felt she was loose enough, he slowly dropped his hands to her neckline and worked his way to the inside of her blouse. She didn't object. Jack even heard her give a tiny sigh as his palms moved over her bare shoulders. He almost sighed himself. She felt like heaven. It was just as he'd thought her skin would feel—warm and smooth, and a bit silky. He could only imagine how the rest of her body would feel. His hands froze.

Easy does it, Jack. The woman made it clear she had a headache. Not to mention a fiancé.

"Sabrina, I found some Tylenol in the back of my desk. I think they're still—" Christine came to a halt in the doorway, eyes wide.

Jack was a lot of things, but not a gambler. However, he would've bet the entire company on what Chris was thinking at that very moment. Hell, he would've been thinking the same exact thing if *he'd* walked in on a man with his hands inside a woman's shirt—as platonic as it was.

Sabrina opened her eyes and seemed to immediately put two and two together. She tried to pull away, but his watch got caught on her shirt collar.

"This isn't what it looks like," Sabrina blurted. She was tugging so hard to separate them, she almost ripped her blouse. *Then there'd be a story,* he thought.

Chris hesitated. "Uh, of course."

"No, really." Sabrina finally was able to break away and stood. "He was helping my head."

Chris licked her lips, trying to hide a smile. "I brought something for your headache, too," she said, holding up a bottle.

Sabrina buttoned her blouse. "Oh, Jack gave me something already."

Chris's eyes danced with amusement as they traveled over to Jack. "Did he now?"

"Ibuprofen," he said with a shrug.

"Well, you're definitely a man of your word." She regarded Sabrina again. "I can see I'm not needed, so I'll just let Jack continue…*helping* you." Chris winked, then rushed out the door.

Sabrina nudged Jack. "Did you see that?"

"Yeah, I saw the expiration date on the Tylenol too. You're going to have to toss it. Now let me finish your massage." He was about to put his hands on her again, but she batted them away.

"No, forget the massage. This is terrible." She pivoted and paced three steps back and forth, all the while rubbing her forehead. "Do you have any idea what a big mouth Chris has?"

"I thought she was your friend?"

"She is. My bigmouthed friend."

"Even better. I was trying to think of a way to spread that rumor without being obvious. We want the office to think we're a couple, remember?"

She frowned. "I know, but—"

"What are you worried about? Your reputation? It's not like we were standing here lip-locked in each other's arms." Not that he hadn't entertained that little fantasy once or twice himself while his hands were over her. Truth be told, he was more than up for the task if she wanted him to make it a reality. Not that she would ever ask him.

Sabrina flopped down in the chair. "But Chris is my friend. I feel funny not telling her the truth."

There she goes again. He figured if he could bottle her neuroses, it would be a hundred times more potent than any stimulant on the black market. "You've had no problem deceiving David. Why is this so different?"

"Maybe because it seems like this thing between us is getting out of control. She should know the truth."

"Absolutely not. The less people who know in the office, the better. Less chance for slipups that way."

Sabrina seemed to think it over. She finally stood, but her eyes still looked worried. "I guess you're right."

"That's my girl." Without thinking, he pulled her into a hug. She was soft and warm and smelled like powered sugar. Then he kept his arms around her, telling himself she needed the extra reassurance.

"You're still coming to David's fund-raiser tomorrow, right?" She drew back slightly and looked at him with eyes the color of a perfect summer sky.

He smiled, but his breathing had taken on a rough edge. "I wouldn't miss it. In fact, I called *Boston* magazine and they're going to be there too. If we play our cards right, we could even end up in some pictures on their blog. So wear something dazzling. Not that you wouldn't look completely ravishing in a Hefty trash bag."

A pretty pink crept up Sabrina's cheeks, then seeming to realize she was still wrapped in his arms, she politely disengaged herself from his embrace. "Well." She cleared her throat. "Good. It seems everything is going according to plan then, right?"

Jack's arms felt empty, and suddenly he was the one who went tense. He jammed his hands in his pockets and scowled. This was not good. His attraction to Sabrina was becoming a complication. A complication he could not afford to act on.

He turned and headed for the door, figuring they both could use a little space away from each other. They'd spend enough time together tomorrow night—time together with her jackass fiancé.

He stopped before heading out into the office and looked back. "Yeah," he finally answered through gritted teeth, "everything is going exactly according to plan."

• • •

Saturday evening Sabrina adamantly searched her closet until her prospects went from good to bad, then steadily approached butt ugly. She had nothing to wear. David had already seen her in that black dress at the Ram's Horn. Then she ruled out a few other dresses because of the weather.

That left her staring at only two would-be candidates. Finally pulling out what she dubbed *old standby*, she vowed to devote next week's paycheck to getting some new clothes. If she wanted to play the part of a woman who captured the interest of Jack Brenner, she'd have to *look* the part.

She held the dress up against the light and inspected the floral silk. *It's actually very pretty*, she thought halfheartedly. The dress was long and flowing, with a low scoop neck and little flutter sleeves. Not exactly sexy, but kind of classic and romantic. Probably a nice change of pace from some of the outfits Jack's model girlfriends had been seen in.

Sabrina finished dressing, and, after examining herself in the mirror, decided to leave her hair down and loose. Her brunette hair settled nicely on her shoulders with little flips at the ends. She glanced at the time, and her heart leaped when she realized Jack would be picking her up at any minute.

"Of course you're happy to see Jack," she told herself as she put on a pair of small pearl earrings David had given to her for her birthday. "He's your friend."

Yes, a friend. She thought again about how sweet Jack had been when he went in search of pain reliever for her headache the other day. She had to chuckle because "sweet" and "Jack" were two words she would've never put together in the same thought a few short weeks ago. Funny how quickly this fledgling friendship was happening between them.

The doorbell rang and, forgoing the perfume she was about to apply, Sabrina went to answer it.

Jack wore no tie but managed to look both elegant and casual in a stone-gray suit. His grin exuded that male confidence of his and a jumpy feeling awakened in the pit of her stomach. She blinked twice and took a step back, wondering if she'd ever get used to Jack's dark, dynamic presence.

As he stepped in, his eyes lit up with pleasure. "You look incredible."

She felt herself beginning to blush, then had to sternly remind herself who she was trying to impress. "I hope David thinks so, too."

Something in his turquoise eyes shifted. "If he doesn't, he's more of an idiot than I already suspect," he said in a voice low and controlled.

Her heart thumped erratically. She forced a smile and tore her eyes away from Jack's penetrating gaze. Why was she so flustered? Did she have to act like every other woman Jack Brenner had ever come across in his life? He meant nothing to her. And she meant even less to him. Jack probably couldn't wait for the day that all this pretending would be over and he could date other women again. Women he really wanted, not just pretended he wanted.

"What's the entertainment for this event?" he asked, breaking her thoughts.

"Broadway by Request."

"As in Broadway musicals?" Jack made a face. "Ugh. Is it too late to cancel?"

"What? You have to go," she said, frowning. "How else is David going to see how well I'm doing without him and want me back? Plus you already called the media."

"Fine. But I can assure you that no straight man will be happy tonight."

"I'll have you know, plenty of heterosexual men enjoy

Broadway music."

He snorted.

"Oh, for goodness's sake, suck it up. This is for *charity*."

"Okay," he huffed. "I'll just sit in the corner and nurse my beer like a good boy."

"There won't be any beer."

"All right, wine."

She shook her head. "No alcohol of any kind. It's being held at the Tradewind Hotel, which used to be a church. I think when the pastor sold it, he had it stipulated in the contract that it would always remain dry."

Jack looked up toward the ceiling and groaned. "If God has any compassion, he'll strike me down now."

She couldn't help but laugh. *Poor guy*, she thought, smiling. He almost looked like he was about to cry.

"Don't be such a baby." Sabrina took a step closer and smoothed his lapels. "Think how good this is going to be for your reputation."

She glanced up, and seeing the cute, cranky demeanor still lingering on his face, pressed her lips to his cheek. "Don't worry. You'll live."

She was about to turn away, but Jack grabbed her hand. "You broke your own rule," he told her with a deep look that sent a tingle through her spine.

"R-rule?"

His lips curved, a devilish gleam in his eyes. "You said no kissing, but you just planted one right here," he said, tapping a finger to his cheek.

She gasped. *Ohmygoshohmygosh.* She did kiss him. Hadn't even given it a second thought. "I…uh…"

"I know," he said, his smile turning steamier than a cup

of hot chocolate in the Arctic. "You couldn't control yourself. I get that a lot. Look, if you want to change the rules, you won't hear any complaints from me. Although you might want to save the good bits for when people are actually around to see."

Her lips thinned. "Bite me."

"Probably a little soon in our fake relationship, but since you asked so nicely, I'll see what I can do when we get home."

She rolled her eyes, then picked up her coat, draping it over her arm. "Let's just go and get this over with before I succumb to my flaming passion for you."

"Right. Wouldn't want you to break any more *rules* on account of little ol' me," he said, batting his eyes at her.

She chuckled as the realization hit her full force. Jack had gotten to her. She was actually falling under his spell like so many women before her. Oh, no. Since when had she become attracted to emotionally unavailable playboys?

Big mistake, Sabrina. Don't do it. Jack Brenner avoided commitment like she avoided meat. If there were ever two people who wanted completely different things out of life, she and Jack would be them. She had to concentrate on David. David, who had the potential to give her what she so badly wanted: a relationship, a family, *a future.*

As long as she was aware of that fact, she'd be safe.

But then Jack slid his fingers through hers as he led her out the door. Goose bumps danced up the back of her spine, and she felt her willpower slip another notch.

Chapter Nine

When Sabrina walked up the stairs, she was in awe of the exquisite dining room. Long rows of tables were covered with crisp white linen cloths, and large ornate candles surrounded by green ivy and white lilies were placed as centerpieces. Even a stage was set in the front of the room with a piano, two Queen Anne chairs, and a settee, cleverly making it look like a small formal living room for the singers.

She handed Jack her coat and was immediately met by David. "Sabrina, I'm so glad you're here. I need you."

Those words would have been music to her ears, except David carried a huge glass bowl and wore a face of sheer panic. "There's no one to go around and collect the song requests," he explained.

Before she could respond, the bowl was plopped into her hands. "Oh. Sure, anything I can do to help," she said, fumbling with its heavy weight.

David's gaze then landed directly on Jack. She frowned

when she realized that David had nothing more to say to her. He didn't even blink at the extra care she'd put into getting dressed for this evening. She thought for sure he'd express some interest or make a small comment.

About to make her way to the tables to collect the requests, Sabrina caught Jack's steely expression and the glare David returned to him and had second thoughts about leaving them alone.

She placed a hand on Jack's arm. "Why don't you come with me?" She phrased it more like a command than a question and tried to get his attention by tugging on the sleeve of his blazer. But he wouldn't look away from David.

"Go ahead, Brie. I'll be fine here." Jack finally broke his gaze away long enough to bend down and gently brush his lips against her cheek.

She had to smile at the use of a nickname in spite of the tenseness of the situation. Jack really knew how to play up the pretend intimacy. But even though he seemed calm and everything was proceeding as planned, her feet wouldn't budge. The way the two men continued to assess each other, she still half expected a high-noon shootout at any moment. Her only consolation was that they were in a former church.

Hearing someone call out that she had a request to make, Sabrina had no choice but to leave. She turned her gaze back to Jack and all but drilled holes right into his forehead, despite the grin she kept on her face. *Jack, do you hear me?* She hoped telepathy would work through his thick skull. *Don't blow this.* Then, praying for the best, she walked away.

• • •

Jack could tell by the way David stood there with his chest puffed out like a rooster that he was itching to have words with him. That's what civilized doctors like David used. Words. But not Jack. He preferred fists, especially when dealing with civilized doctors with puffed chests. Of course, they were at a charity event and Jack couldn't afford the bad publicity. Plus, as much as he would enjoy it, Sabrina wouldn't appreciate him sending her fiancé to the emergency room.

"What's up, Doc?" Jack asked. He inwardly winced. No wonder he did better with his hands.

His question hardly mattered, since David went right to what was on his mind. "What are you doing with Sabrina?"

Jack responded with a lazy shrug. "At the moment, I'd say I'm attending this charity event of yours. It looks like it's a hit."

That comment drew a slow, cool smile. "Yes, but I'm not surprised. The Assist Club does do a lot of admirable work."

"Well, you're an admirable guy."

"You and your father should get involved with the club. The organization provides a lot of great networking. It'll be extremely useful to me when I open up my own practice."

"Brenner Capital gives to many charities in and out of the Boston area. However, we give without expecting anything in return."

David scowled and left little doubt as to his lack of patience with their small talk. "I'd like you to leave, Brenner."

"Sorry, no can do. Sabrina invited me, plus *I* happen to be the kind of guy who sticks to a promise once I commit to it."

David's eyes narrowed dangerously. "Don't give me that bull about sticking to commitments. I know your type. But

Sabrina isn't going to be fooled for much longer. She's hanging on to you now because she's needy and can't handle being alone, but she'll figure out sooner or later you can't give her what she wants."

Jack snorted. "And you can? That's funny, because I don't see your ring on her finger any longer." Although that wasn't nearly as funny as David calling Sabrina a needy person. Just wait until she heard that one. "It's time for you to step aside, Doc, and let Sabrina go. You've had your chance."

David's expression turned a degree colder. "We'll see about that. You're just an infatuation, but she still loves *me*."

Jack watched him storm off, more than sorry he'd kept his hands at his sides. Words were useless with a guy like that. Dr. Personality needed to be knocked down a peg. Or twenty.

He had to find Sabrina. Damn it. She couldn't be in love with that jerk. Was she that blind? He couldn't keep it to himself any longer. She had a right to know what a mistake she'd be making.

Looking around, Jack found her in the corner of the room talking to an elderly couple, and slowly released the breath he hadn't realized he was holding. There was no describing the way his mood lifted when he saw her. Sabrina had the weirdest effect on him, provoking rushes of protectiveness and tenderness and…something else he wasn't entirely sure he liked.

She looked stunning tonight, the way the soft waves of her hair brushed her shoulders and her long dress flowed over her delicate curves. She reminded him of an angel. Sabrina seemed to be everything that was good and honest and loyal. But she was also passionate and fiery. Things that pompous ass of an ex-fiancé obviously didn't appreciate.

Her face lit up as she smiled, listening to every word the couple was saying. She had a smile that drew them in, as it did him. Jack wanted to be over there—just to be near her. Touch her again. It was an odd feeling for him. He was so used to holding part of himself back so he wouldn't ever have to want or need.

We'll see about that.

His jaw tightened remembering David's parting words. Jack couldn't let her go back to a guy like that, agreement or no agreement. This whole jealousy scheme was going on the back burner tonight, he decided, as he made his way through the crowd. Sabrina needed to have her eyes opened.

Jack just hoped she wouldn't hate him in the process.

• • •

Sabrina turned around and ran directly into Jack's chest. "Oh, Jack," she said, "you startled me. Do you have a request?"

"Yeah, I do. It's called let's get the hell out of here."

She smirked. "Nice try. Let me just put in some requests of my own, and then we'll go sit down." She took out a few index cards and began jotting down her favorite songs.

"We're not sitting at David's table," he growled.

She stopped writing and looked up. "Why? You didn't say anything stupid, did you?"

"Why do you automatically assume I would say something stupid?"

She flashed him a grin. "Basing it on your track record."

Jack folded his arms. "Well, *he's* the one who said the

stupid things. You should have heard him. He said—"

"Just lay off, okay?" She shot him what she hoped was a withering glance and picked up the bowl again. "Come on, I have to hand these to the singers." Walking over to the stage, she saw a man wearing a tuxedo and gave him the bowl of requests. Not realizing Jack was so close on her heels, she ran into him again when she turned around.

"What is with you tonight?"

"I'm serious, Brie," he said, taking her elbows and steadying her. "David is not the charitable guy you think he is."

"Look, you promised you'd behave yourself, so just hold in the animosity toward David for a little while longer." She searched the room. David's table was already full, but there were a few seats open at the one next to his. "I see a spot. Come on."

Before they could make a move, a woman stepped into their path, aiming a dark, seductive smile at Jack. "And I thought this event was going to be a major snoozeville. Now that you're here, Jacky, the excitement is guaranteed to pick up."

The woman was beautiful and athletic-looking, reminding Sabrina of a Dallas Cowboys cheerleader or professional volleyball player. By the way she eyed Jack—like a starving man assessing a midnight buffet—Sabrina safely assumed the woman knew Jack well.

"Jessica, good to see you," Jack said in a monotone voice.

The woman ran her fingers up his lapel, then pouted her overly made-up pink lips. "I think you can do a little better than that for an old friend."

Jack hesitated, then leaned in and kissed her chastely

on the cheek. "We need to go find our seats. See you later."

"Wait. A couple of friends and I are meeting at O'Leary's Bar after this. Lisa and Kyle from the yacht club will be there, too. Why don't you join us? I'll have your favorite drink waiting."

"Actually, I can't," he said, drawing Sabrina to his side.

Jessica flashed a grin that probably brought most men to their knees in zero to sixty seconds and toyed with her hair. "Oh, come on, Jack. It won't be the same without you. I'll make it worth your while."

Sabrina's cheeks ignited. It was one thing to have to witness the way women threw themselves in Jack's path, but it was a slap in the face when one knew he was with someone else and still did it. She obviously wasn't deemed worthy competition. And maybe the woman was right on that aspect. After all, Sabrina knew she wasn't Jack's type. But this was the first time she ever truly *felt* that way.

Hot all over with embarrassment, Sabrina tried to free herself from Jack's hold, but his grip grew firmer with her struggle. "If you'll excuse me," she told him curtly.

Jack's eyes burned into hers, but he smiled down at her as if nothing were amiss. "You can't leave without me, honey." He turned back to Jessica. "I'm sorry. I forgot to introduce you two. This is Sabrina Cassidy, my girlfriend."

Jessica frowned, then blinked at Sabrina as if seeing her for the first time, which was most likely true. "Oh. Nice to meet you." She looked back at Jack and pasted on an overly bright smile. "Well, I should go. If anything changes, give me a call. Ta-ta," she said, waving two manicured fingers.

"*Ta-ta*?" she asked Jack, once Jessica was out of earshot. "I can't believe you went out with a woman who uses that interjection.”

"I can't believe I'm 'going out' with a woman who uses the word 'interjection.'" He wove her arm though his and nudged her forward. "You know, you could have played the part of the devoted girlfriend a little better. You backed off me like pork barbecue was emanating from my pores."

"I wasn't sure if you wanted her to think we were dating or not."

"Why would you think that? Everyone *has* to think we're dating if it's going to be believable."

"Well, she's very beautiful. I figured you wouldn't want to miss a chance to meet up with her."

Jack stopped walking and gazed directly into her eyes, his face right above hers. "Believe me, I'm not missing anything. She'll find a replacement for me before this event has ended."

"Then why do you hang out with someone like that if she's so shallow?"

Jack looked away. "Because I'm equally as shallow," he murmured. "Come on."

She was silent as she tried to interpret that. Maybe she would have believed Jack a few weeks ago, but not now. Not now that she knew him better. Underneath that superficial facade he portrayed, Jack was thoughtful and had a sensitive core. Traits—along with his obvious love for his family—she happened to admire about him.

They found two empty seats at the table in front of David's, and it turned out she already knew one of the couples sitting there. As she made the introductions to Jack, he pulled out a chair for her. "Mr. Hubert is the chief of staff at Boston General where David works," she explained, as Jack shook hands with the man.

They sat down, and the waitstaff began serving the different food specialties donated by various restaurants in town. It was family-style, so Mrs. Hubert shifted to pass the scalloped potatoes to her. "I was sorry to hear about you and David, dear," she whispered.

Inwardly delighted to have Mrs. Hubert bring up the topic, Sabrina tried to keep her expression even. "Oh yes, it was very hard. But I'm sure that David and I—"

"Are completely done with each other," Jack supplied.

Mrs. Hubert's gaze traveled over to where Jack was sitting. Her eyebrows raised an inch up her forehead. "How do you know?"

Jack grinned in return. "Sabrina and I are seeing each other now."

"Really?" the woman asked, eagerly leaning in.

"Good timing on my part, I guess. I've been looking—searching—for years for that special someone to settle down with. Then all of a sudden, David gets cold feet, I get a job transfer, and Sabrina and I just clicked. You need to have that special chemistry to truly make a relationship last. That's why Sabrina finally dumped him," Jack went on, swinging his arm around Sabrina's shoulder and giving her a tight little squeeze. "That connection was missing."

Sabrina smiled pleasantly at Mrs. Hubert, even though she felt like biting through steel. *What is he doing?* She wanted to ask him that exact question, but the MC started introductions to the group of singers gathered at the center stage.

The group broke out in a chorus before the piano player randomly picked a song from the bowl of requests Sabrina had collected from the room. Jack slanted her a look when the first song turned out to be "Suppertime" and the singer started off howling and pretending to be Snoopy from *You're a Good Man, Charlie Brown*.

Sabrina chuckled despite the desire not to, then gave him a good-natured poke in the ribs. She knew Jack was more bark than bite, and as much as he complained about coming, he would enjoy the show.

The show did turn out to be very entertaining. And after twenty-some-odd songs and an intermission, the president of the club finally took the microphone, giving a hearty thanks to everyone who helped put the event together, as well as to all the sponsors.

"Now we're going to do something a little different," the president announced. "In an effort to raise our fund-raising quota, we're going to auction off one last song of the winner's choice. I'm sure a few of you out there have a favorite song that you'd still love to hear tonight. So why don't we start the bidding at one hundred dollars."

Sabrina raised her eyebrows. But apparently she had underestimated the generosity of the crowd, because before she realized it, the bid had reached five hundred dollars.

Out of the corner of her eye, she saw David raise his hand. "One thousand dollars," he said.

Sabrina was stunned, and the crowd broke out in loud applause. She knew David was charitable, but that was still a lot of money to donate on top of all the time and money he had already given. She looked over at him and beamed her approval.

"Two thousand dollars," she heard from the deep voice seated next to her. The crowd broke out in applause again.

Her head whipped to Jack. "What are you doing?"

"Bidding on a song," he answered evenly. "Two can play David's game."

"What game? You don't even *know* any Broadway songs."

He glanced over his shoulder at David. "Sure I do."

"But—but you said you don't like musicals."

"Just because I don't *generally* like Broadway show tunes doesn't mean I don't have a favorite or two. In fact, right now, I have a certain hankering to hear something from *Mamma Mia*."

She held a hand over her eyes. "*Mamma mia!*" she groaned.

"Three thousand dollars," David called out.

Sabrina turned and saw him laughing as he received a few hearty pats on the back from the people around him. Above the cheering, he grinned and gave her a confident wink, but she was too concerned about what Jack was going to do next to smile back.

She grabbed Jack's arm. "Okay, that's enough. David's chairman of this event. Don't outbid him."

"Don't worry," he told her, patting her knee. "I know exactly what I'm doing."

Uh-oh. She knew enough of David's personality that he wouldn't tolerate being embarrassed in front of his peers, but for some crazy reason it seemed like Jack was making that his personal mission. "Look, don't—"

Before she could finish her thought, Jack jumped up out of his seat and the crowd fell silent. "I'll donate *five* thousand dollars," he said, aiming his challenge directly at David, "in the name of Brenner Capital Investments."

Sabrina's jaw dropped as the crowd cheered and clapped, clinking their glasses. She slunk farther in her chair. This was so not good. She almost couldn't look at David, but when she finally gained the courage, it was just in time to catch his brooding glance as he allowed the bid to stand.

Unfortunately, that didn't end the commotion in the room, and Jack played up to it by taking her hand.

"Sit down," she snapped, when he kissed the back of her hand to the encouragement of the crowd. Cameras flashed, and she was certain Jack was making sure he not only embarrassed David but assured himself a prominent picture on some society page as well. She was going to kill him.

"My, your young man has certainly made an impression tonight," Mrs. Hubert remarked brightly.

Sabrina couldn't comment. Jack's antics had sucked the ability to form words right out of her. But when she got it back, she was going to make darn sure she made her own kind of impression on Jack.

• • •

"I cannot believe you did that."

Sabrina fumed the whole car ride back to her place, but now that they were pulling into the parking lot of her building, she couldn't hold it in any longer.

Jack shrugged a shoulder as he put the car in park. "It's for a good cause, but if you're feeling particularly grateful, I won't hold you back from showing extra appreciation."

"Appreciation? Ha." After flinging open the car door, she then jumped out. She couldn't believe that Jack thought nothing of his ridiculous bidding war with David. She found it even more amazing that he thought she'd be pleased with that over-the-top floor show he'd provided as well.

"Hey!" Jack sprang out of the car and followed her up to the building. "What's your problem?"

"My problem? You completely embarrassed David— not to mention me. *That's* my problem." She stormed into the building.

She was only a few feet from her apartment door when he grabbed hold of her arm and gently swung her back around again. "How did I embarrass you? I donated five thousand dollars to David's charity. I thought you'd be happy."

"Happy? I told you not—"

The door at the end of the hall opened up and Mrs. Metzger stuck her bottle-blond head out. "Everything okay, hon?"

Sabrina held in a sigh. "Everything's fine. Couldn't be better."

The older woman nodded, smiling at Jack, but took her time closing the door.

"Just go," she told Jack when the woman disappeared. "You're embarrassing me again. My landlady probably has her ear to the door as we speak."

He lowered his voice. "Then let me in so we can talk in private."

"Absolutely not."

"*Please.* Let me explain."

"No. We're done talking."

"I'll sing 'Mamma Mia' at the top of my lungs if you don't," he threatened, amusement in his eyes.

She blinked. "You wouldn't dare."

"Just try me." His eyes narrowed and they stared each

other down for several long seconds. Eventually a laugh bubbled from her lips. Then he laughed, too.

Damn him and his ABBA singing ways. The man was incorrigible. She hated the fact that he had just successfully robbed her of all her fury. Even now as she stood across from him, the humor in his clear blue eyes was swallowing her up. "Fine," she said, making herself sound stern, "you can come in. But this better be quick."

Jack followed her inside and immediately made himself comfortable, taking off his blazer. "Isn't this cozy?" He grinned, rolling up his sleeves. "You can yell at me all you want now."

She wasn't about to let him charm her any further. "Jack, what were you thinking, outbidding David like that?"

"Yeah," he said, looking pleased. "That really got Dr. Too Little."

That remark earned him her fiercest glare.

"I'd say I got off cheap." Jack leaned against the back of her sofa, the corners of his mouth twitching. "Charity donation…*five thousand dollars*. Look on David's face…*priceless*."

"David was donating money to help his organization, not to make you look bad."

"Don't be too sure about that," he shot back. "All David wanted was to look good in front of you and all his networking friends. The guy's a capital *P* phony."

"He is *not*. And whose side are you on anyway? I thought you were just supposed to make him jealous, not go around judging and embarrassing him."

Letting out a huge sigh, Jack stepped closer and placed his hands on her shoulders. "Sabrina, I'm sorry, but I had to do it. You needed to see what a mistake you're making trying to win him back."

She shook off his hands. "You had no right. We had a deal."

Wearily, Jack rubbed his face with both hands. "I know. But...how can you be so sure he's the right man for you?"

She held his gaze a long time before looking away. She had never spoken what she was thinking to anyone. It was almost as if she were afraid she would jinx her own thoughts. But maybe it was time.

Gazing into his compassionate eyes, she took a deep breath. "Well, there are things," she began slowly, "about David, our engagement, that just makes it feel right. Like a sign."

"Sign?"

She smoothed her lips together and went on. "Well, I told you how we met, how great he and his family have been to me. But there's more. When David proposed, he had no idea—still has no idea—but he proposed on the anniversary date of my parents' death. Don't you think all that is more than a coincidence?"

Jack's eyes narrowed, but several seconds went by before he responded. "You want to get married to David because of some crazy *superstition*?"

His reaction caused a wave of heat to radiate from her face. "No, I want to get married because I want a husband and a family. I want to marry *David*, because he's a wonderful man, and I know he'll make me happy." She paused trying to control the cracking in her voice. "Don't you see, it's like he's getting a stamp of approval from my parents somewhere."

Jack turned away and ran a hand through his hair so hard it stuck up at the ends. He quickly turned back. "You've got to be kidding. If your parents are giving that guy their stamp of approval, the distance from up there is clouding their view."

"Madame Butterfly said we would get back together, too. I can't ignore all that."

His mouth drew in a tight line. "That's the stupidest reason to marry someone I've ever heard. I mean, a *sign*? A psychic? Don't you have any sense at all?"

"It's not stupid." Her lips trembled, and she felt tears burning the backs of her eyes, but she kept them from breaking free.

Jack reached out to touch her cheek, withdrawing quickly when he saw her body tense. "Look, don't get yourself—"

"I believe in those crazy superstitions, as you call them. It's all I have at this point, Jack. But you wouldn't understand that, would you?" Her voice was rising by the decibel, but she didn't care. "You have a living family to fall back on for support, to help you, to guide you. Oh, but you never need anything or anyone. All you want from life is your precious work. Well, you—" She hiccupped, then covered her face as hot tears spilled down her cheeks.

• • •

Jack stood helpless for a moment.

Then he walked up and closed his arms around her. Guilt had him swallowing hard as she sobbed, shaking under his hands. He could kick himself. The last thing he'd wanted was to go and make her cry. He just didn't want her marrying

David for the wrong reasons. He was worried about her. That was what he should have told her from the beginning. But no, he'd let his temper control his big mouth again. He was a complete, grade-A jackass.

He held her tighter, and when her crying finally began to quiet, he had already made the decision to bank down his pride. "I'm sorry," he murmured as the light vanilla scent of her hair swept over him.

Sabrina froze for a few seconds, then whipped her head up. "Really?"

"Yeah." He gazed at her beautiful, tear-stained face and his throat tightened. "You're right. I went off script and completely blew our deal. Your beliefs aren't stupid. I'm the stupid one. It wasn't my place to interfere."

"Thank you. That means a lot to me." She gave him a tiny watery smile, and then her gaze wandered to his mouth.

Unexpected, unwanted desire unfurled in his stomach and he swallowed. His heart picked up speed as if he'd just jogged around the apartment building. That was the signal. *Let her go, stupid*. He knew he should drop his arms now and take several steps back. But he didn't.

Couldn't.

"Jack?" she whispered.

He moved his face closer to hers. "Yes?"

"Maybe you should…let me go now."

Her eyes, still shiny with tears, burned into his. When she looked at him like that, so sweet and vulnerable, he became defenseless, too. Something inside him snapped. Before he knew it, his lips landed softly on hers—and by all that was holy, she was kissing him back.

She slid her arms around his neck as he deepened the

kiss. She tasted of apples and cinnamon, courtesy of the apple cider served with dinner, but there was much more to her. Something was different, like the planets were aligning. All because she was kissing him and it wasn't pretend. There was no David watching. Nothing for show this time.

He ran his fingers through her soft brown hair and down her back, gathering her up against him. She fit so perfectly in his arms. His body tingled from the contact. He didn't know how much more he could take and finally, he broke the kiss. "Let's continue this elsewhere," he murmured huskily. Lightly holding her fingers in his, he began to lead her to her bedroom.

Sabrina dug in her heels. "I can't."

Jack turned and studied her. Okay, she did look a little shaky. He was knocked for a loop, too. But not a problem. He scooped her up in his arms and managed to take two small steps before she shook her head.

"No, Jack. I can walk. I mean, this isn't right."

"Of course it's right. It's more than right." He fought the panic rising in his system and swallowed hard. "It's perfect."

The soft, dreamy eyes she'd been gazing up at him now aimed hard and direct. "No. It's not perfect. It's fake."

Her words cut, and just like that reality came crashing back. He allowed her legs to unceremoniously drop to the floor. "It felt pretty real to me," he murmured.

Sabrina drew in a shaky breath as she looked away. "We just got a little carried away." Her gaze managed to travel back to his. "It's only natural. I mean, sometimes being friends with a person can lead you to—"

"You can save the bit about friendship. Trust me, I don't want to touch any of my other friends like I want to touch you right now."

Jack had the satisfaction of seeing color spring onto her cheeks. "Okay," she began tentatively, "I'll admit we do share a kind of…mutual attraction. But that doesn't mean we should act on it." She took a defiant step back, putting a mile of distance between them.

"But we're two consenting adults. There's no ring on your finger, and there's certainly none on mine."

"I know," she began, "there's no ring on my finger, but there's the *hope* that there'll be one again. It's what I've dreamed of having. The whole point of our charade. As much as I'm attracted to you, I can't settle for less than that."

Now Jack knew what she was telling him. He hadn't made it a secret that a long-term relationship wasn't exactly something on his life's agenda. Sabrina wanted a future—with her ex-fiancé. But David wasn't here. And Jack was.

When did something so simple get so complicated?

A small sigh escaped her lips. "Jack, I'm sorry. I don't mean to hurt your feelings."

"I have no feelings, remember?" The way she flinched at his words had him wanting to apologize all over again. *Twice in one evening*, he thought bitterly. That would've been a new record for him.

"I didn't mean—"

"If not you, then there'll be some other woman—like Jessica—before long, right? Is that what you really meant? Look, if you want marriage and the whole nine yards, then that's what you should have. Don't let me or what's happening between us get in your way." Okay, he wasn't handling the situation like he'd wanted to at all, and worse, he was feeling extra cynical, so he picked up his coat to leave.

Sabrina walked over to him and laid a hand on his arm. "It would only complicate our plans," she assured him.

"You're right," he managed between clamped teeth. The last thing Jack wanted was her touching him now. Where her hand gently rested felt like fire going directly to the bone. He was sure by the time he reached for the doorknob his arm would be singed clean off.

Without another word, he let himself out before he did or said something even stupider. Like apologize again. Or worse yet, fall on his hands and knees and beg her to change her mind. *Now* that *would be a new one*.

Hearing the door quietly close behind him, he let out a sigh of relief. At least he was out of there with some shred of dignity still intact. Although his body was in rebellion, he had to admit Sabrina was right. It would've been a big mistake getting involved with someone like her. He didn't do long-term. She was just the kind of complication he'd steered clear of for years. It wasn't part of what he really wanted. All he wanted was to concentrate on his career. He wanted to be back in good standing with his dad and the board. He wanted to take over Brenner Capital. He wanted…

Sabrina.

As Jack started walking down the hallway, he honestly didn't know what he wanted anymore.

Chapter Ten

"I went over a few of your sales ideas, Jack, and I'd like to set up a lunch meeting this week to discuss them with you."

Jack looked up from his desk. Pride filled his chest as he took in his dad's pleased expression. Jack was so close to getting the position he wanted. His ideas *were* good. And if they impressed his father, he knew they'd impress the board of directors. But he'd been working hard on his image as well as his job over the past few weeks. He hoped that part hadn't gone unnoticed, but just to make sure, it was time to use his trump card.

"Sabrina helped with those suggestions, Dad. We've actually been working closely lately—very closely."

"I know." His father's eyes lit with amusement. "She looked lovely the other night at the fund-raiser you two attended."

"How do you know about that?"

"One of the stockholders emailed me the link to the

Boston magazine blog this morning. Apparently, your donation was quite the showstopper."

"Yeah, about that—"

"Well done."

"I— You think so? I know I said the pledge was from Brenner Capital, but I had planned on using my own money."

"You can take it out of the company's account. The Assist Club is a wonderful organization. Very nice idea to have us donate there. That's the kind of publicity I don't mind seeing from you."

"Yeah, well, Sabrina and I weren't at that event for work." Jack cleared his throat. "We're dating now."

His father's grin spread wide, as if it were Christmas morning and he'd just been handed a puppy. "That's fantastic, son. And here I thought you still had the national sales manager position stuck in your head. No wonder you've been working so hard, to spend more time with Sabrina."

"Well, uh, yeah. Of course." Jack fumbled with his words, worried his plan had backfired on him. "Sabrina is great, but Brenner Capital is still my number-one priority."

His dad's forehead wrinkled in a frown. "Oh. I'd hoped this news meant you were making room in your life for more important things than work now."

"What could be more important than our company?"

"*Family* for one thing."

Jack's jaw tightened. "I'll be at Laurie's for Thanksgiving."

"Making an appearance at your sister's house is not what I mean and you know it. Everything revolves around work with you. What would your mother say if she saw you only devoting—"

"Don't go there, Dad. Mom's not here to see or say

anything now because of her own choice." He and his father stared at each other across a sudden ringing silence. Jack swallowed the bitterness in his throat. He didn't mean to sound so angry with his mother, but her suicide still cut deep. She obviously hadn't felt he or the family had been important enough to live for.

His dad let out a long sigh. "I just don't want you to miss out on a good thing when you finally have it. Sabrina is a wonderful woman. Don't go through the motions. Life is too short not to live."

Jack unclenched his jaw. "I *am* living. I'm dating a nice girl, just like you suggested, and I'm even generating good press for the company. I don't know what more you want from me."

"I want you to be happy."

Tightness expanded in his chest, and he looked away. "I am happy."

"You just don't get it, do you?"

Jack got it all right, but he didn't want to admit that much to his dad. It would only prolong the conversation and disappoint his father further. And Jack didn't have the energy. Apparently, he was good in business, but that was all. When it came down to family—relationships—he was a failure. He hadn't been enough for his mom and now it seemed as if he couldn't please his father, either. Even Sabrina had rejected him the other night. Was there any wonder he preferred to invest all his time in work?

His father threw his hands up in disgust and walked over to the door. "Jack, I don't want to fight with you," he said wearily. "But I already lost my wife and sometimes…sometimes I feel like I'm losing my son as well."

· · ·

Sabrina chewed on the end of her pen and stared at her computer. She'd been on the same screen for who knew how long, but she hoped she at least *looked* productive. She was having a hard time thinking about anything other than Jack. Thank God he had an appointment this morning and had been gone before she got in. Maybe he'd be out of the office for the whole day—or if she was extremely lucky, the rest of the week. She couldn't imagine seeing him again so soon after what had happened between them Saturday night. He probably thought she was some kind of tease with all the mixed signals she'd thrown at him. Obviously, spending so much time together outside of work was messing with her brain, and she wasn't acting like herself anymore. She should be concentrating on David. Jack may be a handsome man— she'd even admit he had his moments of humor and kindness as well—but they were completely different people. Different enough to want different things out of their lives. He'd practically said so himself. Jack wanted her, yes, but not for a lifetime. It wasn't a big deal for someone like Jack to have a casual one-night stand, or whatever he was used to having with a woman. But where would that leave her in the end? Probably much worse off than she was right now and nursing *two* broken hearts to boot. She could never be a loner like Jack, and if she wanted to make sure she didn't end up like him, she was going to have to put some distance between them.

"Earth to Sabrina."

She snapped her attention up to Maddie's smiling face.

"Oh. Hey, what are you doing here?"

"We have a lunch date." Her friend raised an eyebrow. "Remember?"

"Oh, right. Sorry. My mind has been…elsewhere." *And primarily on a meat-eating Adonis who only wants a pretend relationship with me.*

"No apologies necessary." Maddie grinned. "As long as you're buying."

Sabrina glanced at her Hello Kitty clock, surprised that it was twelve thirty already. She'd been thinking about Jack for longer than she'd thought. "Okay, but I choose where."

Maddie made a face. "No deal. I want a real lunch. Not just vegetables."

Sabrina took out her purse from the bottom drawer of her desk and stood. "You'd like vegetarian meals if you'd try them," she said in a singsong voice.

The door to Mr. Brenner's office opened and he stepped out. "Hello ladies," he said, offering them both a sunny smile. "Are you going to lunch now, Sabrina?"

She automatically set her purse back down on her desk. "Yes, but if you want me for something, it can wait."

He waved her off. "No, no," he said with a chuckle. "Just wanted to know. When you get back, I'd like to speak with you though."

"If you want to talk now, I could—"

"No, you have a good lunch, sweetie." He shot her a wink, then walked back into his office with a spring in his step that made him look almost two decades younger.

Sabrina and Maddie exchanged curious looks.

"What was that all about?" Maddie asked. "I don't think I've ever seen your boss so happy."

Sabrina nodded. Mr. Brenner's actions were perplexing, but that wasn't what was bothering her. It was because it was the first time he'd ever called her *sweetie*.

• • •

"Come on. Live a little."

Sabrina stared hard at the sloppy, cheese-oozing steak sandwich Maddie held out for her, and shook her head. "No thanks. Why are all of my friends trying to slowly kill themselves with either meat or cigarettes?"

"You have other friends?" Maddie took a bite of her sandwich and grinned.

Sabrina held her stomach in a mock laugh. "That's so funny. You two have the same sense of humor as well."

"Who does?"

Sabrina hesitated, not wanting to mention Jack because she'd felt she'd been talking—and thinking—about him enough lately. She wiped her fork with her napkin and stalled for time.

"*Who* has the same sense of humor?" Maddie pressed.

She sighed. "Jack."

"As in the *Boston* magazine article Jack? As in 'if I were single I'd be all over him like white on rice' Jack?"

"You know exactly which Jack I'm talking about, and I had a feeling you'd make a big deal about me mentioning him."

"Sorry. So I assume you and Jack made nice at work and are BFFs now?"

"Well, I suppose Jack and I have gotten friendlier lately."

"Oh?" She lifted one brow. "*How* friendly?"

"Friend friendly. We're kinda sorta helping each other out, so to speak."

"*Helping* each other? Explain," she prompted.

Sabrina let out a long sigh. "Jack and I are pretending to be in a relationship. For a short time. He needs to change his image at work, and I figured if David got jealous, he'd realize how much he loves me and come back. It's a win-win situation when you think about it—and strictly business. No funny stuff is going on whatsoever."

Maddie looked unconvinced. "Uh-huh."

"No, it's true. You know I'm committed to David. All signs point to him as my soul mate. Besides, it's not like Jack and I are really dating. We're just fake dating. It would never work between us anyway. Jack is hardly the type who wants to be saddled in a relationship or get married."

"So you discussed it then?"

"Yes. I mean, *no*." She shook her head and tried again. "I mean, the point is moot because I'm getting back together with David."

Maddie gasped. "David proposed again?"

She bit her lip. "Well…not exactly. But I feel it's imminent. My seeing Jack is driving him nuts."

"Oh? What does Jack have to say about all this?"

Maddie sounded so accusing that Sabrina sat back and folded her arms. "What could Jack possibly say about anything?"

Her friend shrugged. "I just thought Jack would have an opinion on the whole David situation. With the way you've been going on and on about Jack lately, I thought he might have taken an interest in you that was beyond friendship. But I guess not, since he hasn't even put those luscious lips of his on you. Some playboy, huh?"

"Yeah, some playboy," she said with a chuckle she didn't feel. She shifted in her seat. *Is it hot in here?*

When the silence dragged on, Maddie's eyes widened. "Oh. My. Goodness!" She pushed her sandwich out of the way, then, with a second thought, brought it back and took a hearty bite. "Details," she mumbled, chewing fast.

No house of cards could have folded faster.

"Oh, Maddie, it was terrible," she blurted.

Maddie's mouth dropped open. "Jack's a terrible kisser?"

"Oh, no. He's a good kisser." *Incredible kisser*, she mentally corrected. "But the situation is terrible. I love David, and there I was, all ready to have sex with another man."

"Sex?" Maddie choked. "Whoa." She straightened her shoulders and began fanning her hands in front of her face. "Stop fast forwarding on me. How'd we go from one kiss to sex with Jack?"

"I didn't have sex with Jack. I *would* have had sex with him. I think. At least, I had some good sense left and stopped it."

"That doesn't sound like good sense to me," Maddie muttered.

"Trust me, it is. Jack hasn't made it a secret that he's looking for a brief fling, and David's at least somewhat interested in a relationship. It's not such a tough choice once you step back and look at the big picture."

"Yeah, but right now, you don't have either."

Sabrina couldn't argue with that, and feeling worse than ever, she slumped over her salad with her head held in her hands. Her emotions were jumbled up. She'd thought she had it together going into Jack's scheme, what she wanted out of life: commitment, marriage, family, stability. With David. But now all she could think about was Jack.

Maddie reached across the table and patted her shoulder. "Take it easy, honey. Maybe you're overanalyzing this attraction."

"I don't know," she said with a sigh. "I guess I'm trying to protect myself. At this point, there's no more to think about anyway. Jack and I agreed to just stay friends, which is for the best. I mean, a guy like that hasn't made the Top Ten Bachelors of New England for five years in a row without good reason. He obviously *wants* to remain a bachelor."

Maddie didn't bother hiding the disappointment in her voice. "I suppose that's true. Lucky for you that you're aware of all this now."

"Lucky?"

"Yeah. By knowing everything beforehand, there's no chance you could let yourself get attached to Jack."

"Uh, right." Sabrina felt a knot form in her throat. "Lucky me."

• • •

Jack's door was closed when they got came in from lunch. Uh-oh. He was back from his morning appointment, which meant she'd have to face him sometime today. But first she had to face his father. After tossing her purse inside her drawer, she knocked on Mr. Brenner's door, then took a peek in.

Mr. Brenner looked up, removed his glasses, and gestured to a chair. "Please sit down, Sabrina."

She did, and for the first time since she was hired, felt some unease. "What did you want to talk to me about, sir?"

"I've been seeing good reports on Jack's traveling and sales numbers for you two, as well as some other things I'm very pleased to see."

She let out a rush of relieved air. "Oh yes. We've been working hard to keep our expenses down, too"

"I have a feeling it's all because of you."

She flushed. "I haven't really been doing much. In fact, Jack has been taking all the initiative himself with the territory."

He nodded thoughtfully and folded his hands. "Jack's trying to make a good impression."

"He wants you to believe in him."

"I'm not the one he's trying to impress."

She cocked her head. "I'm not sure I understand."

"It's okay, sweetie. You don't have to hide it anymore. I know exactly what's going on here."

Uh-oh. The jig is up. He'd figured out Jack was trying to look good to the board by pretending to have a serious relationship with her.

"It wasn't my idea!" she blurted. "I didn't want to do it at first."

"You gave him a fight, did you?" He chuckled. "Well, good for you."

She blinked. "You're not upset?"

"Upset? I'm tickled pink. Jack's used to getting his own way. I'm glad you made him work a little to get what he wanted."

Several seconds ticked by. "Mr. Brenner, what are we talking about?"

"You and Jack, of course. But don't think I'm going to go easy on your workload just because you're dating my son." He gave her a devilish grin that instantly reminded her of Jack. She went very still.

"Uh, yes, Jack and I are…" *This was part of the agreement. Play along, stupid.* But for some reason she had trouble saying the words out loud. "Mr. Brenner, I would never ever presume to get any special treatment."

"Now, now, don't get defensive. I know you. You would never do anything like that. That's why I'm so pleased Jack saw all those wonderful qualities in you. I have to tell you, you're exactly the kind of girl I hoped he would start dating. Always seeing those fancy-faced airheads. It's about time he started noticing someone with beauty *and* brains. It will be especially nice for my daughter Laurie to have a female to talk to on Thanksgiving."

"Thanksgiving?"

"Yes. Don't tell me Jack didn't mention Thanksgiving Day plans with you yet. Laurie always has the family at her house for the holidays."

The ground shifted beneath her. "Of course he mentioned Thanksgiving to me," she said with a nervous laugh. "Why wouldn't he, since I'm his"—she swallowed— "girlfriend."

"Excellent. We'll look forward to having you."

Her stomach clenched tight. She hadn't counted on this. More lies.

Silence fell between them as Sabrina gazed into the man's happy face. She didn't have the heart to tell him she wasn't coming to dinner, but finally managed a weak, "Was there anything else, Mr. Brenner?"

"No, that's all," he said, putting his glasses back on. "You keep an eye on my boy and continue showing him what he's been missing out on by always putting work first."

She forced a smile. "Yeah, will do." Somehow she was able to stand, and although her legs were shaky, they got her through the door with some mode of decorum.

Ohmygoshohmygoshohmygosh. She had to talk to Jack. She'd never considered how far their charade might have to go. Now she was expected to go to Jack's sister's house for the holidays? No. She couldn't. She had to draw the line of deceit there. With the steadfastness of a nuclear missile, she dashed across the room and, without knocking, stormed into Jack's office.

"Typically when a door is closed, you knock first," he told her matter-of-factly. "But since you're my adoring fake girlfriend, I'll let it slide this time."

"Shut it, Jack. We've got trouble."

Jack leaned against the back of his leather chair. He met her eyes squarely, but there was a trace of a smile on his lips. "*We've* got trouble?"

"Yes. Your dad wants me to spend Thanksgiving with you and your family."

He cocked an eyebrow and waited. "And?"

"No *and.* That's it. That's the problem."

"That is not a problem. That is a deal-making fact."

She gasped. "You have to change it then. I can't do it. I thought we would just be pretending in public and around the office. But this... I can't go to your sister's home and pretend to be your girlfriend in front of your *family.* I'll screw it up. I'm a terrible liar one-on-one."

Chuckling, Jack stood, then walked over to her. "Calm

yourself," he told her, cupping his palms over her shoulders. "You'll be fine. Tell you what, I promise to keep the nuzzling to a bare minimum if it makes you feel better."

"It doesn't."

He sighed. "Look, Sabrina, you're supposed to be my girlfriend. Where else would you be on Thanksgiving?"

She thought about that with a sinking depression. If she wasn't back together with David by then, she'd spend Thanksgiving alone, probably having Chinese takeout. However awful that prospect was, it still beat lying to Jack's family.

"I don't know." She shook her head so hard she thought her ears would ring. "Make up something. I don't care. Anything. Just get me out of it. *Please.*"

Jack studied her for a long time, his expression leaving her guessing as to his thoughts. Then he reached out and gently tucked a strand of hair behind her ear. "Okay, I'll talk to him if it'll make you happy."

Tension drained from her shoulders, but she still felt the heat on her ear where Jack's fingers had touched. She lifted her hand to it, hoping to stop the sensation. "Th-thank you."

She managed a small smile until she watched him walk back to his desk and sit down. "I mean talk to him *now*," she said.

"Why?"

"Because your dad's been treating me funny lately." *We've been acting funny lately.* "I want it to end immediately." *I want these feelings I'm starting to have for you to end immediately.*

He rolled his eyes and stood back up again. "Okay, if it means that much to you."

She breathed out a sigh of relief. "More than you know."

Sabrina followed Jack out of his office and didn't miss the raised eyebrows Chris shot her from across the room. Choosing to ignore the look, she sat down at her desk and began her work as Jack went into his father's office.

About fifteen minutes passed. She managed to return one brokerage call before Jack stuck his head out again. "Brie, can you come in here for a second?"

She scanned his expression for a verdict of his father's reaction, but nothing registered on her radar. "Everything settled?" she asked slowly.

"Yes—more or less."

She nodded and stood. It took all her courage to walk inside Mr. Brenner's office. She expected to be met with disappointment, maybe even a little anger, but instead, she saw her boss just as happy as he was before. *Huh. Jack must be a real spin doctor.* But then again, Jack was good at sales for a reason.

She cleared her throat. "I guess," she began tentatively, "that Jack explained everything to you."

"Yes, he did."

"Good. I'm so sorry, Mr. Brenner. I should have made myself clear earlier."

Mr. Brenner nodded. "I totally understand. I promise to keep this quiet until you're ready to do it yourself."

She looked curiously to Jack, willing his eyes to hers, but he wouldn't look up from staring down at his stupid cordovan shoes. What would she have to be ready to do herself?

She didn't have to wait long for the answer.

Her boss's smile widened as his arms extended out. Wings of panic started fluttering through her body even before Mr. Brenner pulled her in and enveloped her in a huge bear hug. "Welcome to the family," he said heartily.

Welcome to the family?

Sabrina let that statement hang in her head for several seconds before she attempted to close her mouth and swallow. Then the situation came into focus. She was going to strangle Jack. That was all she could think as she stood embraced in his father's arms. This was *not* correcting the problem. Jack had just made it a thousand times worse.

Mr. Brenner finally relaxed his arms and pulled back to smile warmly at her. "Sweetie, Jack explained how you wanted to keep things quiet because you were afraid how it would look, you know, so soon after your recent broken engagement."

Sabrina saw her boss's mouth moving, but her brain began to pop and fizz like a mouthful of Pop Rocks and she couldn't make out a single word that followed. Jack must have realized it too, because he nudged her waist to get her attention.

"I completely understand why you wanted to downplay the whole thing," Mr. Brenner went on. "But I married Jack's mother after a weekend courtship, so I'm not concerned about you not dating each other long enough." He cocked his head and gave his son a sly look. "Jack's not getting any younger, and I can certainly see why he wouldn't want to wait and let you slip out of his hold."

Her tongue still wouldn't budge. But what could she say? Instead, she pinned her eyes so hard on Jack she thought they'd dart out of their sockets. Jack had the nerve to look confused. Mr. Brenner turned away from them to take a seat at his desk. Taking the unguarded opportunity, Sabrina drew back her foot and tried to kick Jack hard in the shin. But his reflexes were quicker, as he dodged her toe, wrapping his arm around her shoulder and tightly pulling her into his side. She tried to push away but his arms were like a vise. He clamped tighter as she tried to wiggle out, but the minute his father turned around they froze and stopped struggling with each other.

"I knew something special was going on between you two," his father said, waving a finger at the two of them embraced in each other's arms. "But still, this is the last thing I expected so soon."

Jack grinned down at her. "Well, Dad, I think it was the last thing we *all* expected."

She lifted her gaze heavenward. Definitely the understatement of the year.

His father smiled and turned toward her. "Sweetie, maybe it was because of your age or because of your family situation, but I always considered you like a daughter. So you can understand that this is doubly good news for me to hear. I hope you feel the same."

Sabrina's eyes began to fill up. He actually considered her *like a daughter*. Not one of her foster dads had ever said those words to her. But she had always longed to hear them, to feel as if she belonged. Then she remembered that none of this was real. The engagement. The potential family. It was all a lie, and her heart suddenly crumbled into a thousand pieces.

There was no way she could let this charade go on. But

as if sensing she was about to throw herself on the mercy of the court and confess everything, Jack squeezed her shoulder to warn her off.

"I'm a changed man, and Sabrina's the reason," Jack said, grinning down at her. "There's only one woman for me now." He looked as though he was about to kiss her, but she guessed when he saw her snarled lips, he thought better of it.

Wise move, buddy.

"Well, sometimes that's all it takes," his father agreed. "Finding the right woman. We should celebrate. How about you two joining me for dinner tonight?"

That prompted Sabrina to finally find her voice. "Um, Jack," she spoke, looking up at him with what she knew was a saccharin smile, "remember I wasn't going to be around tonight? You know, I have that…*thing*…to…to do." Ugh. She really was a horrible liar. She hoped Jack would follow her lead and at the very least have the decency to get her out of dinner.

Jack caught on fast. "Oh yeah," he let out slowly. "Sorry, Dad. She'll have to take a rain check. We can all celebrate together when we do our big announcement."

Oh yeah, she thought sarcastically, *must do the big announcement.*

"Okay then." Mr. Brenner smiled, clasping his hands together. "You two better get back to work."

Jack pivoted and pulled Sabrina along with him to the door. "Thanks for keeping things quiet for now, Dad." He playfully rolled his eyes in Sabrina's direction. "Wouldn't want to take the wind out of Sabrina's sails. She still has to brag to all her girlfriends."

Sabrina moved fast this time. Freeing her arm, she

elbowed him hard in the side. Jack winced but covered it with a quick grin. "Now I've embarrassed her," she heard him explain as she marched through the door.

Her jaw clamped tight, Sabrina didn't bother stopping at her desk. She didn't even turn around to see if Jack was following. Eyes aimed straight ahead, she ignored the half-dozen heads that turned in her direction, and she marched to Jack's office. Once inside, she fumed and waited. Jack followed a few seconds behind. She whirled around to face him.

Pressing his lips together, Jack raised his hands in a calming gesture before closing the door behind him. "I know you're upset," he began.

She snorted. Loudly.

"Okay, really upset. But I think if you look at it from my point of view, you'll see—"

"*Your* point of view? Jack, we only agreed to pretend to *date*. I asked you to simply get me out of Thanksgiving Day dinner and now your father thinks we're getting married. Oh, and by the way, when you propose, you're supposed to let your fiancée in on it."

He let out a long sigh and when he spoke, his voice sounded low and defeated. "Look, you saw my dad. When I was in his office, he went on and on about us dating and how he was looking forward to Thanksgiving and me settling down. With what he's gone through with his health recently and the argument we had earlier, I just couldn't disappoint him again. A fake engagement is probably the closest thing to a real engagement he's going to get from me. So what's wrong with giving him a little temporary happiness?"

She shook her head. "I don't know…"

"Brie, all I'm asking is that you stick out our agreement

as my fiancée instead of my girlfriend. It's making my dad really happy. Besides, didn't you say David was close to the breaking point anyway?"

She hesitated. The thought of mending her relationship with David was almost an intrusion to what had been going on in her mind. "I—I suppose so."

"There you go. I'll continue to help you if you just let my dad enjoy the prospect of me getting married. At least until the next stockholder's meeting."

"What will you tell him at the end of that time frame?"

"Well, it needs to be a mutual breakup of some sort to look good to the board. Otherwise, I'd make myself out to be the total villain."

"Well, naturally. That's because you are the villain." She tried to hold back her smile, but Jack must have seen it, because he broke out in one of his own.

"I do have a few reputable qualities," he told her teasingly and slid his fingers through hers. "Since you're my fiancée now, maybe you should try looking for them sometime." He raised her hand and held it against his warm lips.

Her flesh prickled at his touch. She couldn't remember her response to David ever being as charged. Was this some cruel trick of fate? She tried taking her hand back, but although his grip was gentle, it was also firm. "Don't—"

"Don't what?" he asked huskily. But he didn't wait for her answer. Instead he turned his attention back to her hand as he lazily drew imaginary designs on her palm. "Isn't this what engaged people do? This is kind of new for me, so maybe you could instruct me better, seeing as how you're the one with all the experience." He looked up, unsmiling and direct. Then his head lowered, his eyes searching.

The door behind them swung open. Although they were both taken by surprise, Jack never dropped her hand as they both turned to see who it was.

"Whoa. Sorry, Jack," the man said.

Sabrina recognized him as Brian Ruiz, the wholesaler to Virginia. Although Brian wasn't in the office on a regular basis, he did stop in from time to time to visit family. He and Jack hung out together at all the regional meetings.

"Doesn't anybody knock anymore?" Jack barked.

Brian's otherwise happy-go-lucky appearance quickly turned into a "man, what's your problem" look. "I did knock," he told him. Then his eyes regarded Sabrina more closely. "Oh, I see," he related with a grin that showed all was now forgiven between him and Jack. "I should have known you wouldn't be wasting any time since you transferred here."

"Not now, Brian." Jack's jaw was clasped so tight, she barely saw his lips move.

"It's okay," Sabrina said as she delicately removed her hand from Jack's. "I was just leaving." She was glad for Brian's interruption, because he was exactly right. Jack didn't waste any time, especially with women. That reminder was the sack of ice in the face she needed.

"Wait, Brie," Jack said in earnest.

"Don't bother asking me for any more *instructions*, Jack," she told him with a thin smile. "I'm afraid you're going to have to rely on your own instincts from now on." Opening the door farther, she sidestepped Brian and left.

• • •

Sabrina didn't go directly home after finishing work. Something about what had happened with Jack today, something that went beyond asking her to pretend to be his fiancée in front of his father, bothered her. Jack had looked as if he was about to kiss her until Brian Ruiz arrived. Would he have? She couldn't be sure. And if he had, would she have kissed him back, knowing there was no future in it? Yes, of that she was sure. And there lay the real problem. She had hoped a drive around the coast would clear her head, but instead she just felt more confused about the situation and her feelings toward David and Jack.

It was almost seven o'clock when she pulled into her condo parking lot. Debating on ordering a pizza, she approached her front door when Mrs. Metzger called her name out from down the hall. "You're getting home late, hon."

Sabrina bit down on a retort, since she knew it was her situation with Jack and not really Mrs. Metzger that put her in such a poor mood. But the woman did seem to have some sort of sixth sense when it came to her comings and goings.

Sabrina nodded politely and continued to stick her key in the door.

"I thought I'd mention that your fiancé came by here looking for you."

Sabrina tiredly looked over. "Which one?"

"You have more than one?"

She shook her head. "Never mind. Did David say what he wanted?"

Confusion still lingered on Mrs. Metzger's tan, wrinkled features. "Well, no. But I wanted to remind you that you can still come with me to my son's house for Thanksgiving." A twinkle grew in the woman's eye. "Unless of course, you're

really spending the day with that beefy new boyfriend instead."

Sabrina smiled, knowing she was referring to Jack. "No.
I think I want to spend it alone." *And think.* "Really," she
insisted when she saw the doubt in her landlady's eyes. "But
thanks anyway."

The woman shrugged. "Okay. You know where to find
me if you change your mind."

Sabrina watched the woman walk back to her apartment
and gave a little wave to her before they both disappeared
through their own doors. She couldn't help but wonder what
David wanted to talk to her about. Did he want to spend
Thanksgiving together? She hung up her coat and fought
the indifference she felt about that.

This should be good news, she reminded herself. David
could be back here with her soon enough. She'd have everything she ever wanted. Her life would be full again, and the
loneliness would be gone. She'd have the prospect of a real
home and children.

But those images were quickly pushed aside for the one
of Jack, and how tenderly he'd gazed at her today.

Chapter Eleven

While he waited for his dad to change for dinner, Jack propped his feet up on the leather ottoman and scowled. He didn't like the way he had left things with Sabrina. She had to hate him after what he'd been putting her through. But she wouldn't hate anyone. Would she?

Leave it to me to test her level of benevolence. He let out a low, bitter laugh.

He'd known she wasn't going to be thrilled with what he'd told his father—no real surprise there. Man, with the way she'd reacted you'd think she had to pretend to be engaged to the spawn of Satan. But she didn't understand. His dad still felt Jack wasn't doing enough to change his image. If only Sabrina had been there and had seen how his father had taken the news, the way his dad laughed and slapped him on the back. The proud look in his eyes. He and his father were finally on the same page, something they hadn't shared since he moved back to the Boston area—maybe even since before his mom had died.

Unfortunately, that wasn't the only reason he didn't tell his dad the truth. Jack was still figuring out what to do about his attraction to Sabrina. He wanted her, yet she loved that asshat of a fiancé. No, she couldn't really love that guy—not with the chemistry she and Jack generated every time they just stood in a room together. And if Brian hadn't interrupted them, Sabrina's lips would have been under his and they would have made plans for the weekend together. But no. She was obviously too blinded by superstitions and how "kind and perfect" David was, which was complete and utter bull. So maybe part of Jack had wanted to see her reaction to being engaged to him, wanted to know what she thought about being with someone like him. Even if it was just pretend.

Well, you got your answer, jackass, didn't you?

She definitely wanted the prick doctor. Sabrina was too loyal. He couldn't imagine what it would be like to have that kind of devotion from a woman—from her. But damn if he didn't want to find out. They still had some time together to play along with this charade. Then he'd have a chance.

A chance at what?

He liked her, yes. He wanted her, yes. But then what? They'd ride off into the sunset on a white horse? Hardly.

Maybe.

He honestly didn't know anymore. That's why everything that came out of his mouth was all wrong. He didn't know what he was feeling. But every time he even thought about her marrying a guy like David, it left him so tight in the chest he could barely take a breath.

"Jack, what's the matter?" His father chuckled, coming

into the room. "You look like Sabrina just dumped you. I wouldn't worry about her going back to her old fiancé now. She's completely smitten with you."

Jack's hands closed tightly into fists, knowing that was nowhere near the truth. "Yeah, smitten," was all he could manage.

"You ready to go to dinner?"

Jack tried not to make a face, but the knot he was feeling in his chest was slowly traveling to his stomach. "In a minute. Can I ask you something first?"

His father sat across from him. Folding his hands in his lap, he slid his graying brows up expectantly.

Jack didn't exactly know how to start, so he decided to jump in with both feet. "Do you ever regret marrying Mom?"

"*What*?" his father sputtered in surprise. "What kind of question is that? What's the matter with you?" he demanded. "Do I regret marrying your mother? What a question."

Jack shrugged helplessly. "I mean, do you think... investing your love in her was worth it?"

Their eyes suddenly locked and realization crossed his father's features. "Jack, you talk of love like it's a business merger. Are you asking this because of Sabrina? Are you worried about something?"

"Maybe," Jack hedged. *Worried?* He wished. What he was feeling for Sabrina scared him down to his boxers. Who knew the words "I'm engaged" wouldn't make him hurl? And here it was five hours later and he was still fine—not even a hangover effect. It should have been harder.

"I'll always cherish the time I had with your mom. Even the harder times during her depression and then her eventual passing. But I loved her," he said simply. "Plus I got two great kids out of it. I'm disappointed and sad, but not sorry."

"You're not sorry even though she let us down?"

"She didn't let us down. She let herself down. But don't think for a second that she didn't love us. She did. But her inner battles were stronger than any of us realized, and she cut herself off from the joy that was yet to come in our lives. I was a little afraid you were cutting yourself off too—in a different kind of way—with work and the crowd you were running around with. I'm glad that you've opened yourself up to someone like Sabrina instead."

"Do you see someone like her and someone like me together? You know, for the long run?"

His father's eyes narrowed. "You didn't say anything stupid to her, did you?"

"No, I didn't say anything stupid," Jack echoed irritably. *Jeez, doesn't anybody trust what comes out of my mouth anymore?* "I just mean…" He gave up and shook his head miserably.

His father stood and patted him on the shoulder. "Buck up, Jack. I believe what you're feeling is growing pains. A little late for them, I might add. But I wouldn't worry about Sabrina. She's a good egg. Now let's go grab some dinner. I want to talk more about that incentive program you mentioned for the internal wholesalers."

Jack stood up and froze. Technically, that was Sabrina's idea and not his, even though she gave it to him to use. It was a perfect opportunity to shine in front of the board, since his father seemed so 100 percent behind it.

This is it, Jack. This is what you want. Take the reins and lead yourself to the top of the company.

He gazed at his father, waiting patiently at the door, and

realized that changing his image for his father and the board wasn't the only thing he wanted to do. He wanted Sabrina to look at him differently, too. She had told him in the past that he didn't listen to others enough at work. That he was too much of a loner. Maybe she was right. Maybe he didn't listen to her enough, either.

But if he ever wanted to compete with David, it was about time he did.

• • •

"Hi."

Sabrina jumped at Maddie's voice and accidentally punched an extra number on the fax she was trying to send. "Oh, poo," she muttered. "What are you doing here, Maddie? I don't have time to play. Some of us are employed." *For now anyway...*

Sabrina took a deep breath. *Relax*, she chided herself. *No one in the office knows anything. As far as everybody is concerned, you're blissfully in love with your business partner. You're not deceiving your coworkers. And you certainly weren't thinking of Jack Brenner this whole entire never-ending weekend.*

Rrrrright.

Maddie placed her elbows on the table and closely watched her as she retyped the number in the machine. "That was cold. Chris buzzed me in. For your information I *have* been looking for work, and all I said was hi. What's the matter? Did you have a bad weekend? Or is Jack not behaving like the good boyfriend he's supposed to be?"

Sabrina looked at her in horror. "Why? What have you

heard?"

"I didn't hear anything. I was visiting my sister. Did I miss something?"

"No," Sabrina murmured, pushing the send button on the machine again. "Just continue to act like it never even happened."

"What never happened?"

"Exactly."

Maddie huffed out a frustrated breath. "Are we doing an Abbott and Costello routine? What are you talking about?"

"Nothing." She sighed. "Just forget it. I don't want to talk about Jack." She winced as soon as his name left her lips.

Maddie's face lit up. "Oooh, what about Jack don't you want to talk about? Spill."

Sabrina leaned in closer and lowered her voice. "Well, okay. Mr. Brenner kind of got this crazy idea that Jack and I are…*engaged*."

"How in the world did he get that idea?"

"Jack told him."

Maddie blinked. "But you're *not* engaged to Jack. Technically, you're not even engaged to David."

Sabrina flung her hands in the air. "Don't you think I know that? Jack caught me at a weak moment so I agreed to pretend to be his fiancée now."

"Did he get down on one knee at least?"

"Maddie, this is serious. I don't need this right now." *Especially after being plagued with images of Jack all weekend.* She'd already been berating herself since Friday for almost kissing him again and for being such a fool as to begin to fall for Jack's smooth act and lies.

Maddie chuckled. "Okay, okay. Sorry. Does David

know?"

She shook her head. "No. There hasn't been any formal announcement yet."

"That's good. You're a *terrible* liar."

Sabrina narrowed her eyes. "I know you mean that as a compliment."

"Of course," Maddie said with a grin. "Well, this is an interesting predicament. You are engaged to one man while trying to become engaged—or *re*engaged—to another. I wonder if this is the journey Madame Butterfly told you to enjoy."

Sabrina rolled her eyes. "Oh, yeah. Being with Jack has been a real thrill ride." Although truth be told, any moment with Jack did leave her about as breathless as a roller coaster.

"Thrilling enough to give you second thoughts as to who you want your real fiancé to be?"

Sabrina looked away. "I know exactly who I want." *I think*. "David even left me forget-me-nots by my door this morning to let me know he'd been thinking about me— about us. Our future together. Wasn't that sweet?"

Maddie said nothing for several seconds, then hugged her. "Sabrina, I want you to be happy, and if you still love David, then I'm rooting for you two. Truly. But I wanted to give you this. I think it's pertinent for the week." She pulled out a piece of newspaper and handed it to her.

"My horoscope?"

Maddie tapped the Sagittarius column. "Read."

"*Confusion could cloud a decision if it is made immedi-ately.*" She gasped and looked up. "Oh my gosh."

"Keep reading."

"*Sit on the matter for a few days, if possible. A partner*

will appear more cheerful than he or she has been in a long time. Know that a boss or older relative might expect certain things from you. Tonight: Go for an early bedtime." She lifted a withering gaze to Maddie. "It was dead-on until the early bedtime part."

"Depends on who you go to bed *with*," she said with a wink. She pulled out her cell phone and checked the time. "I gotta run. I have an interview in forty-five minutes. In the meantime, don't make any rash decisions…about anything."

"All right. I have to get back to work anyway. Thanks for this," she said, waving the horoscope.

"My pleasure. We need to grab dinner and schedule another Madame Butterfly session soon."

Sabrina couldn't help glancing at her bare ring finger. She let out a sigh. "Yeah. Very soon."

• • •

Sabrina snuck a peak in Jack's office as she walked back to her desk. He wasn't there. Not that she was surprised. She'd glanced at his schedule earlier today and saw he had a lunch appointment in New Hampshire. It would have been nice to talk to him, though—just to make sure everything was okay between them. She hadn't seen or heard from him since Friday. But work came first with him. Wasn't that one of the points of this whole fiasco? Jack needed to be out there traveling to show his dad he was working hard, so he could get the promotion he wanted.

So why did she feel so…disappointed? It was no biggie if she didn't talk to or see him today. No problem at all. No problem, except that she kind of—in a very small, innocent way—missed him.

And if she were being completely honest with herself, she missed him more than she missed David.

"Sabrina, can I see you a minute?"

She looked up at Mr. Brenner and pasted on an eager smile, despite the fact that he was still calling her sweetie and it reminded her of the lie every single time he used it. "Sure thing." She just prayed he wasn't going to ask her where she and Jack had their bridal registry.

Closing the door behind her, she saw him gesture for her to sit down. "Sweetie, I'll cut to the chase."

Please stop calling me sweetie! I'm a terrible person. I'm not going to be your daughter-in-law. I'm going to yank your feelings right out from under you, and you'll have another angina attack—or worse—and then I'll be a murderer as well. You should fire me!

"I'm giving you a raise," he finished.

She blinked. "What?"

"I've decided to give you a raise."

"No!" she burst out. She stood up, but not knowing where to go, flopped back down again. "Mr. Brenner, you can't do this. Don't do this."

"I can and will do it," he said with a chuckle. Rubbing his chin, he eyed her with amusement. "You're way too modest. No wonder Jack fell in love with you."

Waves of nausea crashed into her stomach, and she had to close her eyes. Mr. Brenner didn't understand his son at all. Little did he know how far Jack was from being in love with her. "Mr. Brenner, please don't give me a raise because I'm engaged to your son."

"Don't be silly. But Jack does indirectly have to do with

it."

"What do you mean?"

"Well, he told me Friday night at dinner about your idea. About how you thought we should be compensating his internal wholesalers for their help in acquiring sales. It's a great incentive plan. I'm going to get it rolling after the next quarter."

She was speechless—not because Mr. Brenner thought her idea was good, but because Jack hadn't taken the opportunity to claim the idea as his own. It certainly would have made him look even better in his father's eyes and to the board.

So, why didn't he?

"Jack told you that?" She wasn't actually asking a question, but trying to digest the whole idea in her brain. She didn't know what was going on anymore.

"Yes, he told me Friday night at dinner. We missed you, by the way. Did you have a nice…*thing*?

Sabrina knew she had given him a lame excuse for not coming out to dinner with them and as a result couldn't quite meet his eyes when she answered, "Oh, yes." *If you call eating half an anchovy pizza all by yourself and watching a Star Wars marathon on TV until you were so exhausted you had no choice but to finally fall asleep. Then yes, it was quite nice.*

"Good." He smiled. "Incidentally, Jack mentioned he wanted his territory cut once you're married. I guess he doesn't want to travel as much then and be separated from you as often. Poor guy's heart probably wouldn't take it."

Poor guy's heart? Jack pining away for her? Now that was funny. Only she couldn't laugh. Maybe she should share that one with Jack's friend Brian. He'd probably find it hilarious too, especially after what he'd said about Jack not wasting any time with women. Jack certainly wasn't wasting any time playing up their fake engagement.

Hearing enough, Sabrina stood and tried to draw some resemblance of a smile onto her lips. "Thank you, Mr. Brenner, but don't worry. I know for a fact that your son has a very strong constitution."

• • •

It was almost four o'clock, and Jack was still out of the office. He hadn't even phoned in.

Sabrina thought about calling him, but she knew he hated to be interrupted when he was on the road. So she'd have to wait. It was just that Jack's recent behavior didn't add up. Not after everything she'd come to know about him. He'd already shown her that he'd say and do almost anything in regard to keeping on top in his career, including fake proposing to her. Except this time. And now because of that, she was getting a raise.

Tearing her eyes away from Jack's door, she grabbed a stack of notes on her desk and began to sort through them. When she came upon his business expense report, she stopped and stared at it. He would need to sign this — eventually — to make sure he'd get reimbursed. Tapping her pen on her lips, she thought that maybe she should go and hand deliver this to Jack's desk, so it wouldn't get lost. Not that she was exactly going to snoop while she was there, but maybe there'd be something that would give her some sort of clue into her fake fiancé's psyche.

• • •

Jack stood in the doorway of his office and bit down on a laugh. Sabrina may look the part, but she was hardly a Charlie's Angel.

There she stood with a stack of papers held high in one hand while the other hand casually flipped through the notes he'd left on his desk with the other. He had to give her credit, though. If anyone else had walked in on her, or walked by the office, they would've easily thought she was dropping off some papers for him.

But he knew better. And yet he wasn't angry. Sabrina wasn't the nosy type, so he liked the fact that she was interested enough to look through his stuff.

In fact, he liked it a lot.

He slammed the door behind him. "Hi, honey. I'm home."

"Jack!" She turned white and began fumbling with the picture of his parents she had just picked up off his desk. Apparently deciding to save it from falling out of her grip, she took hold of it with both hands, causing the papers to go flying. "What are you doing here?" she said, out of breath.

He leaned his back up against the door, caging her in. "I think that's my line." He grinned. "Find anything interesting?"

Sabrina quickly put the picture back down and blinked up at him like a cornered mouse. "I — I was just delivering…" She stopped as she looked at her empty hands in horror.

"By your feet," he supplied.

"Oh, right." She picked up the papers and held them out triumphantly. "These."

Ah, the perfect picture of innocence. Man, if that didn't draw him to her even more and make him want to take her in his arms. As a result, he didn't dare move a millimeter. "You know, you don't need an excuse to go through my things. I have nothing to hide from my fiancée. There's even some things I'd like to show you, if you'd let me."

"You should really work on that shyness of yours, Jack."

He let out a laugh. "I've never had any complaints about that before."

A flash of annoyance crossed her pretty face. "As much as I'd like to talk about your love life, I actually want to talk to you about something else."

"Okay, shoot." Continuing to lean on the door, he crossed his arms. "You have my full attention."

"Did you know your father's given me a raise?" she said crossly.

He raised his brows. "No, but judging by your reaction, it obviously wasn't a large enough one."

"It's not that. He's giving me one because of what *you* told him. About my idea for compensating the internal wholesalers."

His hands went into his pockets and he hiked his shoulders. "So?"

"Jack, why did you tell your dad that?"

"It happened to come up at dinner. When he expressed interest, I mentioned it was your idea. No big deal."

Her lips parted. "But it was the truth."

He hesitated, trying to clear away the anger he felt boiling up his throat. She really did think he was a spawn of Satan. "Yeah well, not everything that comes out of my mouth is a lie."

"It's just...that was your chance. You could have taken the credit and used it in front of the board."

His gaze seared into hers. "Is that what you'd expected me to do?"

"Well, no," she said, furrowing her brow. "I…I don't understand."

"What's so hard to understand? It was your idea, and you deserve the credit. This company is really lucky to have you." *David's really lucky to have you.* "Maybe it was about time I drew the line and told the truth."

"Does this mean you want to come clean about the fake engagement too?" she asked.

He quickly raised spread hands. "Whoa, whoa. Let's not go nuts. You only got a raise. I didn't get my promotion."

"Of course, where was my mind?" she said wryly. "But thank you. I suppose you are making some progress." She set the papers down on his desk and walked up to him. When he didn't move, she raised her eyebrows, signaling him to step away from the door.

He still didn't budge and hoped she didn't notice him sniffing her hair. "You think I'm making progress?" he asked, enjoying the scent of vanilla and strawberries.

She looked confused at first. "Well, I don't think you're at altar-boy status."

"I'm not looking to be an altar boy or even as perfect as your David. Just trying to polish the old image."

"Keep polishing," she said, grinning. "I think you missed a spot."

He chuckled. His heart warmed at her smile and that maybe she'd seen and approved of something he'd done. It was ridiculously small, but it was a start.

There was a comfortable silence. Just the sound of his pulse pounded in his head as they stood there smiling back at each other. But Jack didn't reach for her. He wanted to, and had to practically gnaw his own arms off to keep from doing so. *She's not yours*, he reminded himself. He knew how she wanted to keep things, so he had to wait if he was going to do it right this time and make sure she was completely over David before he made his move.

Sabrina finally cleared her throat. "I guess we both have work to do," she hinted.

His feet felt like they were in wet cement, but he managed to pull away from the door. He didn't want her to go just yet, but they did have to get back to work.

She opened the door and started to step out, but then stopped herself short. When she looked back, it was with dark, grave eyes. "Thanks again, Jack," she said quietly. "I appreciate it."

Do you really love David? Are you feeling what I'm feeling right now? Things could be so good between us if you'd only give us a chance and forget about David and those crazy superstitions. Those were all the things Jack wanted to say.

"You're welcome," came out instead.

Chapter Twelve

Sabrina flipped through the TV channels as if she were on autopilot. She had no idea what she was looking for, but she didn't want to be reminded that it was Thanksgiving Day—and she was spending it alone.

It could be worse, she reminded herself. Thanksgiving was really minor in the grand scheme of holidays. She didn't even eat turkey. However, it meant Christmas was right around the corner, and that one, she knew all too well from experience, could be downright brutal.

She hit the remote several more times until she found herself back at the Macy's Thanksgiving Day parade. There was no way around it. Mass media was not going to be her friend today. In frustration, she clicked the TV off and hurled the remote. Going back to bed seemed the best option. It wasn't like she'd be seeing anyone.

Bang, bang, bang. The firm rapping at the door had her burrowing deep into the groves of the cushions.

Correction. She wasn't *supposed* to see anyone. She was afraid it was Mrs. Metzger trying to convince her to spend Thanksgiving with her and her family again. But Sabrina didn't want to impose on them or even Chris. Everyone was very considerate and oh so sweet to her, but she didn't want to feel any more out of place than she already did. She had gone through enough of that not-belonging feeling growing up.

Another knock sounded. Bracing herself for her land-lady's niceties, she dragged her feet to the door and swung it open. But the person standing there was the very last one she expected to see.

"Jack." His whispered name was all she could manage, since the air felt kicked out of her lungs.

He looked so perfect, dressed in tan pants and an olive, ribbed sweater. She was half stunned to see him at her door but also half charmed because he was holding a single red rose. Even her knees weakened as he shifted closer to lean a shoulder on the door frame, and she caught the familiar scent of his shampoo. Then those baby blues of his locked on hers and her heart did a somersault.

Uh-oh. She wasn't supposed to be excited to see Jack, not when there still could be a chance with David. Right? No, she could not let herself fall for Jack. She was stronger than that, stronger than her hormones. She could resist him.

His devastating smile was proving more difficult, though.

Pointing the rose at her, he grinned wolfishly. "You're still in your pajamas."

Her head snapped down. Damn. She forgot she still had her candy-cane-striped flannels on. *Doesn't it just fig-ure?* Someone like Jack probably had women answering the door in lacy undergarments and hair-thin thongs. But not her. *Noooo*. Here she was, looking about as appealing as Mrs. Claus after an all-nighter.

"Yes well, it *is* a holiday," she huffed, trying to hide her mortification. "I'm off the clock. I can dress however I want."

Laughter showed in his eyes as he brought the flower up to his nose and breathed in its scent. "You'll get no argument from me. However, as charming as you look, you can't come to my sister's house like that."

"That's fortunate, because I'm not going to your sister's house."

He stilled. "Oh? You have plans with Dr. Wonderful?"

"No." She sighed. "David never called."

"Good. You have to come with me then."

"Uh, you're taking this fake fiancé stuff too far. I don't *have* to do anything."

"Yes, you do. You have to come to dinner with me."

"What? I thought you got me out of going to your family's place."

"I never said that. Didn't you get my text? My father will think it's suspicious if I show up for Thanksgiving without my fiancée." He pointed the rose so hard at her, she thought the bud was going to fly off. "What will I tell him?"

The bubble of him showing up at her doorstep because he wanted to spend time with her officially popped. She was a fool. Jack wasn't interested in being with her. He was only concerned about appearances with his family. Now she was glad she was in her pajamas and only wished they were baggier.

"I don't know what you'll tell him, Jack. But I have full faith that you'll come up with something brilliant to save face. You always do. We're done here." She started to close the door, but his hand shot out against it.

"Hey, you can't break up with me yet. We have a deal."

"Well, our deal is not working, as you can plainly see by my attire and lack of David's company."

"You said you'd give me time," he protested. "The stockholder's meeting isn't for another three weeks. You can't give up now."

She folded her arms and gave him her best "just watch me" look.

"Look, David was getting into his car when I pulled up. He had his hospital gear with him. So I guess that means he's working today?" She didn't confirm or deny his question, partly because it was news to her—but it did explain why David hadn't invited her to dinner. Not that she was really upset at that. She was more upset with her growing feelings toward Jack and what she should do about them.

Jack's mouth twisted, misreading her silence. "Who cares what he's doing today anyway? You don't need him when you have me. Let him eat hospital cafeteria food. My sister is a fantastic cook, and I know my father would love to see you."

She bit her lip and thought about her other prospects— which were exactly none. "I don't know…"

"Okay, forget all those other reasons then. Come for me. This may not mean a whole lot to you, but I'd want you to spend Thanksgiving with me even if we didn't have this deal between us."

She tried, but failed, to keep the surprise off her face. "You would?" She gazed up and into his eyes. There was no way she could misread the genuineness she saw in them.

He tilted his head, then traced a finger along her cheek. "Please come."

Her resolve deflated like a leaky balloon. Jack was becoming harder and harder to resist—in more ways than one—and she nodded a yes.

"Besides…" His expression turned playful as he looked around. "Why am I still out in the hall?"

She blinked. Then, opening the door wider, she stepped back as he waltzed in and thrust the rose into her hand.

"Gee, Jack," she said, biting down on a smile, "while you're polishing your image, maybe you could polish your manners too."

He took off his jacket and shrugged sheepishly. "Sorry. I took your advice and am going meatless for a little while—even today of all days, so help me. I'm a little on edge."

"With your personality, I hardly noticed."

Jack brushed off her comment with a deadpan look, but as she continued to stare at him, she noticed that he seemed troubled.

"Are you feeling all right?"

He ran a hand over the light stubble on his face and sighed. "Yeah. I had a doctor's appointment last week and was told my cholesterol was a little high, which is another reason why I took your advice."

She walked over and rested her hand on his shoulder. "It's great you're taking your health more seriously." He gave her a stiff nod, so she judged he was having a tougher time than he was letting on.

"Have you tried Field Roasts?" she suggested.

He rolled his eyes. "No. I can't remember what I had but it tasted like crap. I don't know how you survive eating this way."

She stifled a laugh. "You get used to it when you start seeing how much energy you get. I'm excited just thinking how good your body's going to feel."

Something flashed behind his eyes and she saw them turn dark and sexy. "Oh, yeah?"

Realizing her slip of the tongue, she sprung her hand back as if his body had turned to fire. "I...I meant that"— she cleared her throat with a cough—"your body is getting healthier as we speak."

A wicked grin appeared on his lips as he closed the distance between them. "I suppose that's one way of putting it."

Heat flooded her cheeks, and her brain became pudding as his finger toyed with the lapel of her pajamas. But she had to be strong against this six-foot vegetarian temptation of a man. Squeezing her eyes closed, she willed herself to step away. And to her surprise, she did. Like ripping off a Band-Aid, only the sting still lingered. It was better to do it now, because if she let herself succumb to Jack's charms, it would hurt much worse when he was done with her and she was alone again.

"I'll go get ready," she said, hoping to change the subject. "We should probably take two cars in case you want extra family time alone." Jack didn't say a word, but as she walked past him to get to the bedroom, she noticed the same broad grin still lingering on his face.

"Oh, Sabrina," he drawled.

She stopped and warily looked back. "Yes?"

His mega-grin grew and was now up to a million watts. "I'm excited just thinking about how good my body's going to feel too." Then he broke out into laughter.

With a groan, she ducked into her bedroom and slammed the door.

• • •

Jack's sister, Laurie, lived about twenty minutes north in Marblehead. It was a small, picturesque town on the coast that still maintained its colonial houses and tight, winding streets that were there before the Revolutionary War.

Pulling up behind Jack's SUV, Sabrina took in the large home with lots of graying cedar and pretty window boxes that reminded her of the ones she'd seen on Martha's Vineyard. There wasn't a lot of property, but she noticed that hadn't stopped them from squeezing a good-sized swing set in the yard.

Jack walked over to her car and opened her door. "This is great. Wait till you meet everybody."

Everybody? The chicken inside of her was beginning to peck its way out. "Uh, maybe this was a mistake. I'm going to stick out like a Yankees fan at a Red Sox game."

"How many times do I have to tell you to relax?" He grinned, pulling her up to the porch. He knocked on the door, but not waiting for anyone to answer, turned the knob and ushered her in.

Sabrina heard children giggling as soon as she stepped in the house. That, and the aroma of pumpkin-pie spices and turkey, warmed her heart, reminding her of what she always wanted her future home to be like on Thanksgiving. She felt a small ache at the reminder that she wasn't any closer to having those things for real.

A tall, attractive woman in heeled boots appeared in the foyer entrance. Her eyes lit up when she saw Jack. "Bubba!" she cried.

Bubba?

Sabrina glanced over her shoulder for some other person in the room, but the woman jumped directly into Jack's arms and hugged him tight.

"I'm so glad you've moved back," the woman said, grinning from ear to ear. "Why haven't you visited before now?"

Sabrina had no doubts at all that this woman was Jack's sister. Her dark hair, cut in a practical, chin-length bob, swung against her cheeks as she assessed the appearance of her brother. She was dressed in jeans and a maroon cardigan, yet somehow managed to maintain an air of sophistication.

"I'm sorry," his sister said, turning smiling blue eyes in her direction. "Here I am rude as can be and having diarrhea of the mouth, all because I'm so excited to see Jack. You must be my almost sister-in-law."

Sabrina glanced at Jack, then smiled weakly. "Must be."

"Well, I'm Laurie." Without warning, the woman pulled her into a warm hug—something Sabrina was finding the family was big on. When she let her go, Laurie automatically turned to punch Jack in the arm. "Why did you wait so long to bring her home to meet the family?"

Jack hung an arm around Sabrina's shoulders and brought her against his side. "I had to make sure she could handle your cooking."

Laurie shot him a mock glare. "How do you stand him?" she asked Sabrina with a hint of a smile. "He's been here exactly two minutes and I've already had my fill of him."

Ꞙiancé Ᏸy Ꞙate

Sabrina smiled politely and hoped Laurie really wasn't expecting an answer.

"Dad here?" Jack asked.

"He's in the family room with Jay and Gretchen."

"Where's Mike?"

"You know my husband's MO. Called away on an emergency C-section. But he promised to be back before we cut the pie."

Laurie turned and led them into the next room where Sabrina saw Jack's dad reclining at the TV watching his grandchildren play video games. The family all looked up when they entered the room, and the children squealed with delight at the sight of their uncle Jack.

After all the introductions were made, Jack sweetly kissed the top of Gretchen's head and playfully shoved Jay on his side in greeting, then walked over and shook hands with his father. Then before she knew it, Jack flopped down on the floor next to the kids and picked up a video controller.

Her boss greeted her with a hug of his own and sat back down. "I'm glad you could make it. Wouldn't have been the same without you this year."

Sabrina's insides melted at his warm welcome. She couldn't remember the last time she'd felt like this. She gazed around at Jack's family with longing. Such a lovely illusion, being a part of this. Being with *Jack* like this. She had spent the holidays with David's family just last year, but it hadn't registered until now how different things were with them, and the thought concerned her.

"What the hell is *this*, Laurie?"

His sister planted an angry fist on her hip. "Dad, will you

tell Jack to watch the language in front of my children?"

"If Dad knew anything about video games, he'd understand the severity of the situation. Still *Super Nintendo*?" Jack said the word like he had swallowed an anchovy. "Come on, it's prehistoric. They might as well be playing *Pong*."

"For your information, I don't want my kids to be a slave to video games. They do *not* need an upgrade."

Jack glanced at his sister, then with a devilish grin, leaned in to the children. "Don't worry," he said in a stage whisper, "I'll hook you guys up at Christmas."

Laurie's eyes narrowed to two fine slits at the children's cheering. "I can't wait until you have kids. No offense to you," she said, turning to Sabrina, "but it's only right that I get to submit your children to a quarter of the abuse my kids have to endure with Jack as their uncle."

Our children? Sabrina felt she must have turned twelve shades of pink and was probably now working on a very becoming hue of magenta.

"Come here, Brie," Jack called to her, patting a space on the floor. "Let me show off for you one of my many talents."

Shrugging helplessly at Laurie, she squatted down next to him.

"This is *The Lost Levels*," he explained, "one of the more challenging of the Super Mario games. You have to go through the maze and fight a dragon at each level."

"You've been hiding this studly manliness of yours." She faked a sigh. "I had no idea how lucky I was."

A slow smile curved his lips. "You ain't seen nothing yet. I rescue the princess every time I play."

"You look like a princess," Gretchen told her in a small voice.

Sabrina turned her head and smiled. "Thank you."

"Did Unclc Jack rescue you from a mean old dragon?" the little girl asked.

Sabrina glanced at Jack and caught his grin that spread from ear to ear. "Well, not exactly. In fact, some people even mistake your uncle for a dragon," she stated with amused satisfaction.

The young girl's eyes widened. "They do?"

"Ah jeez, Gretchen, she's kidding," Jay told his sister. "You know, a joke."

Laurie hooted with laughter. "Your uncle Jack did look like a dragon, especially when he used to puff on those cigarettes of his. Thank God he gave those up."

Jack shot his sister a deadly look. "It's not the only thing I've given up. Sabrina is a vegetarian and has convinced me to cut back on my meat consumption because of Dad's heart issues. For a little while, anyway," he muttered.

"Yeah, right," his sister mocked. "Even your precious beef jerky?"

Jack nodded. "I'm a man on a mission."

Laurie's laughter died, and she exchanged surprised looks with her father. "Well, then. I'd say Sabrina deserves a medal of bravery for that feat," she remarked, not hiding her admiration.

"Oh, no," Sabrina protested. "I really didn't have anything to do with it. All I did was tell him that if he cut meat out just one day a week, it would be good for his heart."

Laurie snorted. "Yeah well, my husband's a doctor and said the same exact thing. Jack never listened to *him*."

"That's because he's not half as pretty as Sabrina." Jack grinned, taking Sabrina's hand in his and raising it to his lips.

"Besides, now that my future is looking brighter, I decided I might as well live a little longer to enjoy it."

Sabrina frowned as she eyed Jack. Did he want to live longer for *her*? She was afraid she was reading into things that weren't there. She couldn't be sure. Their game was going further and further out of her league, and she didn't know how to play anymore. Jack still had not let go of her hand, and the way he was gazing at her made her feel like he was talking about more than just a future within his father's company. It was almost as though he was talking about a future with her. A concept that—if she were being honest—wasn't so foreign from her own thoughts lately.

• • •

After dinner, everyone except the children decided to wait before having dessert and returned to the family room to watch college football.

Before they could get comfortable, Leonard Brenner turned to his son with a gleam in his eye. "Jack, I brought that little item we were talking about before. I thought maybe you'd want to show it to Sabrina now."

Jack turned to her with a sly grin, then wiggled his eyebrows up and down. "Interested?"

Sabrina couldn't help but chuckle. "Why not?"

Jack took her hand and led her upstairs to a guest bedroom. She looked around and didn't see anything out of the ordinary, unless she counted how unbelievably neat it was.

"What did you want to show me?" she asked, feeling a little nervous now that she and Jack were alone.

Jack picked up a black velvet box on the bureau and

caressed it as he spoke. "Now, don't get yourself all worked up about this," he warned. "You worry about things too much. Just look at it and tell me what you think."

When he proceeded to open the box, her brain locked in neutral. "Oh, Jack," she finally whispered. Shaking her head, she wrapped her arms around herself to rein in the distress she felt.

"See?" His forehead wrinkled in a deep frown. "I knew your anxiety level would spike over this."

She tore her eyes away from the two-carat diamond engagement ring in Jack's hand and swallowed. "This is going too far. I cannot believe you bought me a ring."

"Don't worry, I didn't."

She was finally able to take a breath. "Thank goodness."

"It's my mom's ring."

"Your *mom's*?" Her head felt like it was pumped up with helium, and she needed to sit down.

Jack flopped down on the bed next to her. "What's the matter? Don't you like it?"

She still couldn't get her bearings. Maybe she needed to lie down. "Like it? What's not to like about it?"

He seemed pleased with her reaction and took the ring out of the box to shine it against his pants. "Well, you might not like this sort of thing if you're a minimalist," he said with a wink.

"I can't wear it."

Jack's grin dissolved. "How do you know? You didn't even try it on yet."

"This is too much. Your mother's ring should be saved for the woman you *really* want to marry. Not for the sake of keeping up appearances to your family and work-related acquaintances."

He regarded her through heavy-lidded eyes. "This ring's been sitting in this box for years. I guarantee it won't be seeing any action other than your finger."

"Jack, never say never."

"No, I'm sure. I couldn't think of a better person to wear it—even if it's only temporary." He lifted her left hand and gave it a gentle squeeze. "Go ahead and try it on."

She hesitated, then slipped the ring on. She had never seen a more perfect piece of jewelry in her entire life. It was exactly what she would have picked for herself and so unlike the elaborate design David had surprised her with. The ring may have belonged to Jack's mother but Sabrina felt as if it had been made for her instead. And it meant even more to her that Jack entrusted her to wear it. "It's lovely." Her breath caught.

His gaze on hers was so intense, she wanted to look away. "No, *you're* lovely," he said huskily.

"Jack—"

"No. Don't—don't think this time. Not now. Let's just go and enjoy the journey. Wherever it leads."

Journey? She pulled back slightly. "What did you say?"

He shook his head. "My words aren't important. What is your heart telling you?"

In those few seconds, she did listen to her heart.

And then she kissed him.

They clung to each other and fell back against the bed—not in the heated frenzy she had expected, but in a slow, fluid motion, as if every second counted and they needed to silently convey that to each other. She didn't want to think about the make-believe as his lips pressed deeper onto hers. She was drowning in him and couldn't stop herself. Maybe it was seeing how he acted with the children and his family, or just how much fun they'd had together this last month. She didn't know. All she knew was nothing felt as right in her life. She wanted to forget about getting David back and about the superstitions. Could this be her fate, that everything was supposed to lead her to Jack, to this very moment?

"Whoops," Laurie yelped from the doorway.

Jack lifted his head and let out a swift curse. Sabrina's cheeks ignited as she retucked her blouse.

His sister laughed but covered her mouth too late. "I know what you guys were doing was G-rated, for now…but I'd like to keep it that way with the kids around."

Jack sat up and aimed sharp daggers at her with his eyes. "Can't I have even one minute alone with Sabrina? She is my fiancée."

"I don't care if she were your wife. This is my house, you knucklehead. Besides, I need help in the kitchen."

"I'm not helping you clean up," he spat. "Not after this."

"Good," his sister snapped back. "Because I was going to ask Sabrina."

Sabrina blinked. "Oh, of course." She began to slide away from Jack, but he snaked his fingers around her wrist.

"Hey, are we okay?" he asked, his gaze searching.

She hesitated, then kissed his cheek. "Yeah, we're okay." But that wasn't entirely true. Things were different between her and Jack now. She wasn't sure how deep her feelings ran, but she couldn't run from them any longer—which was probably what Jack expected her to do, since his eyes were still trained on hers when she reached the door and looked back at him.

Her pulse whipped wildly. The pull to him was so strong,

she wondered if there weren't actual cords tethered between them. She sent him a reassuring smile.

His lips parted, but Jack didn't smile back. Instead, he studied her as if weighing a deep decision. Before she knew it, he stood and was cradling her face in his hands and looked ready to kiss her again.

"There, there, lovebirds." Laurie hooked an arm around Sabrina's waist and drew her away from Jack. Laurie made a *tsk*ing sound. "Try to survive, big brother. I just need her for a little while. Besides," she added with a grin, "it's not like I interrupted anything out of the ordinary between you two."

· · ·

Laurie placed a pot in the sink and showed Sabrina where she kept the Tupperware containers. "So have you guys set a date?"

Sabrina almost choked. "Uh, no. We—we haven't talked about that yet." They still needed to discuss their actual feelings.

"I have to admit," she confided to Sabrina, "I was absolutely stunned when Dad told me Jack was getting married."

She could relate to the feeling. "Yeah, I know I'm not exactly Jack's type."

Laurie turned to her in surprise. "Oh no, you're Jack's type all right. Except you're missing the 'please insert brain here' sign on your head." She laughed and turned to squirt more soap on her sponge. "But that's not what I was talking about. I just never thought Jack would ever get married. Gosh, the women he went through. For years, Dad's been giving him the responsibility lectures. You know, settle down, grow up, it doesn't look good for the company, yada yada. Then all of a sudden, Jack gets this full turnaround in attitude. It was too convenient. Naturally, I thought it'd be just like him to be putting us on."

When Sabrina spoke, her voice wavered. "You thought he'd do something like that?"

"Oh yeah—not maliciously, of course. I guess it's from being in sales," she said with a little shrug. "He can put on a good act for the sake of the company and especially to get Dad off his back." She turned to Sabrina and playfully elbowed her in the side. "But now I know I was being silly and not giving Jack enough credit. I'm so glad he met someone like you."

Sabrina tried to smile, but her lips felt like they had five-pound weights attached to the corners. Jack *could* put on a good act, apparently. He'd made her feel like she was becoming part of his family for real and not using her for the company's sake. He'd made her believe that it was possible that he had started to have feelings for her that went beyond mere attraction. And she had come to care for him.

How could she let herself forget what Jack's true priority was? After all, he'd been up front about that from the beginning. Despair and loneliness rose within her. It swirled and expanded, making it difficult to breathe. She should be used to rejection, but she was actually trembling now. Their deal and his promotion be damned. She wouldn't be a part of his lies anymore.

She glanced up at Laurie, a heavy feeling in her stomach, and summoned a quick smile. His family was so nice and trusting, she hoped they wouldn't be hurt by her and Jack's actions. But she needed to get away from him, before she was buried any further in deceit. Before he caused her any more pain than he already had.

. . .

"The key is to not stand for more than two seconds."

His nephew nodded at his advice and tried to dodge around Jack to get to the net. Jay told him he wasn't the tallest on his travel basketball team, but he was wiry and fast. All true. But not that fast.

Jack snatched the ball away from him and turned to shoot. When the ball bounced off the rim, Jay pumped his fist in the air and cheered.

"Okay, hotshot," Jack said with a chuckle, "let's work on your three-pointer now."

The side door opened and Jack's dad stepped out onto the back patio where they were playing. "Hey, Jay," his father said, "your mother needs help in the kitchen cleaning up."

Jay groaned but tossed the ball to Jack and ran inside. Jack tucked it under his arm and was about to follow, but his father raised a hand. "Actually, I wanted to talk to you in private. Here is as good as any place."

Jack zipped up his jacket and sat down on the picnic bench next to him. "What's the matter, Dad?"

His father smiled. "Nothing's the matter. That's what I want to talk to you about."

"Okay, now I'm confused."

"You're one hell of a wholesaler, son. Your sales are fantastic and now with your recent engagement to Sabrina, the board is extremely pleased. I'm happy to tell you that you will be the new national sales manager. Congratulations."

Jack blinked, slowly letting his father's words seep into

his brain. When it finally registered, his pulse kicked up and his breathing became labored. Jack had done it. He had finally gotten the promotion. What he'd wanted from the very beginning. It was almost too hard to believe.

He grinned at his dad. "I'm really getting the job?"

"Yes, the promotion *and* the girl, apparently. You're a lucky man," he said, slapping Jack on the back.

Yeah. He was a lucky man. Damn lucky. But only because after that incredible kiss they'd just shared, he knew there would be no way Sabrina would ever go back to David. She was almost Jack's. But not quite. There was no doubt by the end of this evening, she would be, though. He stood, wanting to share his good news with her.

"Thank you, Dad," he said, shaking his father's hand. "This means a lot to me."

"You're welcome. Too bad you'll have to tell Sabrina later."

"Right, I—" Jack frowned. "Later?"

His father nodded. "Because Sabrina isn't here, remember? You never told me she suffers from bad headaches. Poor thing did look pale when she left."

"Uh, right. Headache. I—I forgot she left," he lied.

Jack's mind raced. There was no way Sabrina had a headache. In the span of thirty minutes? So why the hell would she just pick up and leave—and worse, without telling him? A feeling of dread began to unfurl in his stomach. Something must have happened. And he had to find out what.

He turned to head into the house. "Thanks again, Dad. I, uh, am going to go help Laurie too."

"Jack," his father called out as he reached the last step.

His anxiety level through the roof, he spun around to

face his dad. "Yeah?" he huffed.

"Everything okay between you and Sabrina?"

Jack forced a smile. "Everything's fine."

He hoped.

Jack opened the door and scanned the street for Sabrina's car, hoping she'd come back. "What did you say to drive her off like that?"

His sister's mouth dropped open a full five inches. "*Me*? I didn't say anything. I like her."

"Then why did she leave without saying good-bye to me?"

She snorted. "Well, obviously you did something. It must have been a whopper, too. Stay here and give her time to cool off." When he still looked skeptical, she added, "Trust me, I know women. I happen to be one."

"Yeah, maybe you're right," he mumbled. Jack sat down on the step and rubbed his forehead. He couldn't make sense of her leaving. He tried calling her but she wouldn't pick up. Finally, he sent her a text asking if she was at least okay. All he got back was: I'M FINE. WILL SEE YOU MONDAY AT WORK.

Monday? He'd hoped to spend the weekend with her. He thought Sabrina understood that she was becoming important to him. They had fun together. She had accepted his mother's ring and had kissed *him*, really kissed him. In fact, he was convinced she hadn't even thought about old what's-his-name today.

What went wrong?

"Wow, Jack."

He pulled himself out of his misery and looked up at Laurie. "What 'wow, Jack'?"

"You've got that melancholy, woe-is-me look. I wouldn't have expected you to become such a softy when you finally fell in love with a woman."

He stared at his sister, trying to register her words. *Fell in love? Me?*

Laurie chuckled. "You look surprised."

Yeah, he was.

"It's refreshing to see this side of you," she commented. "But I guess love is a powerful emotion. Personally, I became a klutz around Michael. Oh, and the dinners I burned because I was so nervous cooking for him. You just never know how falling in love will affect you."

Jack's heart thudded. Twice.

He was in love with Sabrina.

It all made sense. How he felt when she was in his arms. The way he couldn't get her or her bossy opinions out of his mind. The way he wanted to personally hospitalize her pansy of an ex-fiancé. He quit *meat* because of her.

"I'm in love." Equal parts panic and wonder engulfed him.

"With the woman you're engaged to be married to? I would hope so," Laurie mocked.

Jack slowly nodded, realization sinking in deeper and deeper. Yes, he needed to spend the rest of his life with Sabrina. He actually wanted to marry her. For real. And he needed to tell her.

"Yeah," he breathed. "I'm really in love."

The corners of his sister's mouth lifted with amusement. "Well, *duh*."

Chapter Thirteen

Jack's heart slammed against his rib cage as he approached Sabrina's door. His nerves were getting the better of him, but he couldn't waste another second. He had to let Sabrina know how he felt.

A glance at his watch told him it was almost noon. The same time as yesterday when he had shown up at her door to invite her to Thanksgiving dinner with his family. Before he realized how much he wanted to spend the rest of his life with this woman. Now all he had to do was knock and tell her. Instead he just stood there, his arms paralyzed at his sides. He studied the grain in the wood door, psyching himself up. A second glance at his watch told him he had wasted two minutes.

Okay, stop being a putz. This should be a piece of cake. He'd faced many a surly stockbroker during his business travels and had always convinced them to use Brenner Capital investments. Obviously he'd have no trouble convincing the woman he loved to marry him for real.

He imagined she'd look at him with those incredibly beautiful blue eyes, her glossed, full lips parting in surprise. She'd be thrilled to see him and give him one of those shy smiles that would always twist his gut—the way she'd looked at him yesterday when he'd shown up at her door.

He'd tell her he was sorry for what he had done to cause her to leave his sister's house. Sabrina would forgive him— being the sweet, compassionate woman she was—and he'd pull her into his arms and kiss the breath right out of both of them. *I love you* would spring from his mouth, and she'd scrap whatever plans she had for the day—for the better half of the century—and spend it making love with him instead.

That did it. The image of Sabrina lying in his arms was all the confidence-bolstering he needed. His arm shot out, and he knocked.

Sabrina answered the door immediately, as if she'd been expecting him. Or more likely someone else, because although she wore the surprised look he expected, she was far from happy to see him. In fact, many emotions seemed to flicker over her face in that brief second, but he was pretty sure none of them was joy—at least as best as he could see, since she only cracked the door open three inches. The confidence he'd always prided himself on slipped a notch.

"Jack, what are you doing here?"

Oh, man. Not even a hello. His confidence slipped another notch.

"I wanted to make sure you were okay." He smiled at her, hoping she'd smile too and invite him into her apartment— then into her life. None of that happened.

He cleared his throat. "And I wanted to apologize for

whatever I did to make you run off."

The line of her mouth didn't bend, and he still remained standing in the cold, empty hallway. If his confidence fell any further, he'd trip on it.

"You didn't do anything out of the ordinary," she said. "I figured I fulfilled my part of the bargain long enough."

Bargain? Did he misinterpret their kiss yesterday? He suddenly became tongue-tied. The situation was not going down as he'd planned. She hadn't even removed the chain on her door yet.

"We need to talk. How about letting me in?"

Sabrina paused, then with a small sigh lifted the chain from the door and swung it open. He was slightly disappointed she wasn't in those baggy pajamas of hers this time, but she looked good. *Too* darn good for wearing jeans and a red turtleneck, almost like a schoolgirl with the way her dark hair was smoothed and tucked into a matching headband. So tidy and orderly. So Sabrina. It made his hands itch to pull her close and rumple her all up.

"Jack, I really don't have a lot of time. David will be here soon."

"*David*? What the hell does he want?" She flinched, and he realized too late that he had shouted the question.

She looked at him without her gaze quite reaching his own. "Well, our plan obviously worked, like you said it would. David wants to get back together." She hesitated. "Isn't that great?"

Jack didn't answer. He was way too stunned. But he imagined if he could croak something out, he would have told her it was about as great as a kick in the crotch. And about as unexpected as one, too. It left him standing there like an idiot, waiting for his tongue to shed a couple of hundred pounds so he could speak.

David wanted her back. *Of course* he did. What man in his right mind wouldn't want her back? It was just that the whole time he and Sabrina had been putting their plan into action, Jack hadn't ever really counted on it actually working. David didn't love her. Not the way Sabrina deserved to be loved.

Damn. Jack shouldn't have listened to his sister. He should've gone after her last night.

Gazing at her beautiful face, Jack searched for a clue as to what to say or do next. He noticed how tired her eyes seemed, almost as if she'd been crying. *Tears of joy*, he thought grimly. It made him want to break down and cry himself.

What was he supposed to say now? *I know you have trouble believing anything that flies out of my mouth these days, but don't marry the man you think you love. Marry me instead.*

Yeah, that would go over *real* well.

What could he do? This was what Sabrina had wanted from the beginning, wasn't it? She'd made that clear enough to him on many occasions. She believed fate had led her to David. As much as it killed him, he was going to have to suck it up and do the noble thing. The funny thing was he didn't realize until now he had anything virtuous like that in him. No, he wouldn't make trouble for her. He'd step aside and let her be happy, even if it meant his own misery. Even if it meant her marrying a jerk-face man, getting pregnant, and having a bunch of tiny little baby jerk faces.

His jaw grew tight. It was affecting him like nothing ever

had, so instead of wailing, he did the next best thing. He got angry.

"Congrats," he said tightly.

She looked away. "Thank you."

"So when did all this good news take place? Before or after you put your tongue in my mouth?" Why should he bother hiding his sour attitude? He had nothing to lose now. Sabrina had already decided he wasn't the better man.

Her body stiffened like stone. "Do you have to be crude?"

"Sorry. I'm just trying to put the sequence of events together here. Because you had me fooled. I never guessed you still wanted David after last night's kiss."

Her eyes finally flashed to his, heated and firm. "Give me a break, Jack. I'm not as good an actor as you are. It wasn't like that. David had been trying to get ahold of me all week. We finally talked this morning. The hospital has been pretty hectic lately."

David talked to her this morning. And that quickly, they were back together. Jack wondered if he'd told Sabrina how he felt sooner, if it would even have made a difference. He was guessing not. Jack was just the side attraction. Dr. Too Good was the star of the show. He was an idiot to think she'd see something better in him and forget that fact.

"So he's been busy at work, huh?" he asked. "A lot of people suddenly having heart trouble?" That didn't sound so far-fetched. His own heart was suddenly experiencing some weird pangs, too. "Is that some kind of *sign* to you, too?"

She gathered her arms together and hugged herself. "I don't want to argue about superstitions. There's no point. I just want you to know that I'm really grateful to you for giving me a wonderful Thanksgiving and for all your help. Your…friendship has meant a lot to me. More than I can say. But we both knew the reasons we got into our agreement in the first place, and now, thanks to you, David's realized how he truly feels about me." Sabrina paused and bit her lip. "Was there something else you wanted to talk to me about?"

Jack almost laughed out loud. She had no idea how close he'd come to making a fool of himself. How he'd almost declared love to a woman who wanted to marry someone else. He had to hand it to himself. When Jack Brenner decided to take the big plunge and fall in love, he did it right.

He heaved a frustrated sigh. "Yeah, I wanted to tell you that my dad is giving me the promotion I wanted." He should've smiled when he told her that, but he felt dead inside. The news was pitifully secondary to what he'd really come to share with her.

Her face lit up with pleasure. It was the kind of reaction that tore at his insides, since it was for the wrong reason. "That's so wonderful. Congratulations. Did you mention to him that we wouldn't be getting married?"

He shook his head. "Don't worry. I'll figure out something to tell him and the board soon enough."

"Right." She frowned. "Well, I guess you'll be wanting this back." She took his engagement ring from her pocket and held it out to him.

His misery was a lead weight. He stared at the ring, knowing that when he took it back his fantasy would officially be over. So he waited an extra beat before finally reaching for it. "Yeah, you don't want David thinking he lost his chance. That I beat him to the punch." She didn't crack a smile, but then again he knew his joke was flat before it left his mouth.

"If you want me to be there whenever you break the news to your father, I will."

"No. I got us into it on my own. I can get us out of it on my own, too. I'll take him to dinner on Friday and tell him then."

She nodded and silence fell between them. He took the opportunity to scan every perfect feature of her face, from her sky-colored eyes, to her short, straight nose, to her full and beautiful mouth.

It was excruciating.

Things wouldn't be the same, and he wasn't sure how much more he could stand. It was torture looking at her and knowing she'd never let him touch her again—real or pretend.

"I should go," he finally said, reluctantly tearing his gaze away and walking to the door. He was halfway through it when she called his name.

He turned around, and she rushed up to him with wide, probing eyes. "This is good, right?" she asked. "I mean, we both got what we wanted."

He waited a moment before answering. This final lie was going to be one for the ages. Sabrina didn't need him messing up her plans, and he certainly didn't want her pity.

"Yeah." He fingered the engagement ring a moment, then slipped it into his pocket. "Looks like we both got exactly what we wanted."

She nodded, her gaze falling to the floor. "I guess we did."

• • •

"What's the matter, darling?" David asked. "Are you feeling all right?"

Sabrina looked up from her left hand where David's engagement ring now sat and fought the urge to throw up.

"I'm fine." She tried to smile. "I just can't believe this is happening."

The reality of her feelings jarred her like a car alarm going off in the middle of the night, and she stared at the man across from her as though he were a stranger.

"Well, believe it." David smiled, pulling her close. "I was a fool to think we weren't right for each other." Tilting his head, he kissed her fully on the lips.

She tried not to stiffen, but feeling his mouth pressed against her own made it all too clear that something was different. It wasn't like how she'd remembered his kisses. In fact, if she had to describe it now, it was a lot like kissing a pillow—soft, not totally unpleasant, but still a little…strange.

Oh, no. What had she done? She wasn't in love with David anymore.

She was in love with Jack.

Two months ago she would have been doing an all-out, full-on happy dance around her apartment at the mere *hope* of her and David getting back together. Now she only felt the raw sores of an aching heart—and on the verge of tidal wave after tidal wave of tears.

She'd been afraid her feelings for Jack were getting out of control and thought she'd done her best to protect herself. She even thought her feelings were skewed after seeing Jack this afternoon. But she was too late. David's kiss and seeing his ring sit on her finger, with what felt like the weight of a bowling ball, made her realize it even more.

She pulled out of David's embrace and resisted the urge to wipe her mouth. "Um, why didn't you think we were right for each other?" she asked, trying to collect the gamut of emotions running through her system.

David raised his brows at her question and stared at her as though he didn't exactly know the answer. He turned away and poured them both some wine.

She studied his back and didn't blame him for not knowing. Maybe he'd felt back then what she was feeling right now. That what they had was just companionship but not a real connection. Jack had mentioned that, but she hadn't wanted to listen to him at the time. She couldn't accept his opinion that David wasn't part of her fate. At the time, her judgment had made perfect sense. But now Jack had gone and thrown a monkey wrench into her beliefs.

Jack.

He'd seemed so selfish to her at first. But then she'd really gotten to know him. Although career-driven, Jack had a soft heart for his family. He'd been kind to her, too, and even had the ability to make her laugh—when she wasn't ready to kill him. And now she'd fallen in love with him. The only problem was Jack didn't love her, let alone want to marry her.

As much as she hated the alternative, she knew she couldn't marry David now. She didn't love him anymore. There was a part of her that feared she had never loved him, that she'd fallen in love with *the idea* of him as her destiny. Which made her wonder, was she so blinded by what she thought was fate that she'd ignored her own feelings? If so, she deserved to be alone. She was a total head case.

David took a sip of his wine and smiled. "I thought I'd

just about go nuts when I thought that Jack Brenner, of all people, was winning you over." He shook his head in disbelief. "*Anyone* but him."

She regarded him more closely. "Was that why you wanted me back? Because you didn't want Jack to have me?"

"N-no," he stumbled. "Of course not." He gave her a half-embarrassed smile, almost as if he'd realized his slip. "That's ridiculous. I told you I want to marry you. We belong together."

She calmly put down her wineglass and decided she was finally ready to hear the truth. "Why did you break up with me?"

With a fidgety hand, David took his wineglass and tossed the liquid back like a shot. "Um…well, darling, don't take this the wrong way, but you were getting a little obsessive with the whole marriage thing. I thought maybe you were depending too much on me. It was stifling."

Her eyes narrowed. "So you thought I was clingy and needy?" *Oh no*, she thought, holding her forehead in her hand, *that's exactly what I was. Maybe even still am.*

"No," he said, then seemed to think his answer over. "A little bit." He spread his hand up before she could speak. "But now I know you aren't like that. You got involved with that Brenner guy pretty fast. Almost too fast. That's why I was concerned at first. But then I realized how strong of a woman you are and how you weren't relying on either of us for anything. You seemed so independent and passionate. It was so unbelievably attractive." A smile slowly spread across his lips. "I couldn't resist you after that."

She closed her eyes and groaned. No wonder she was attracted to David at first. They were *both* head cases.

"Do you love me?" she asked softly, already knowing the answer.

"What?" he half laughed. "Sabrina, I care deeply for you. We'll make a great team. I can't imagine marrying anyone else."

Opening her eyes, she repeated, "Do you love me?"

"I…" He paused, raising his wineglass again, and frowned when he saw it was empty. "I think so," he said into it.

She slowly nodded.

Her gaze went to her left hand, and she studied the ring glistening in the light. It was so ornate, certainly not as beautiful as the one that had been Jack's mother's.

This is quite the dilemma, she mused with more calm than she thought she'd have at a time like this. A man who didn't love her wanted to marry her, and the man she loved didn't want to get married. Oprah herself would be chomping at the bit to get ahold of this story. She wished her parents were alive so they could advise her, though in her heart she already knew what to do. Right was right, even if she didn't like what it meant for her future. But she had to take this chance and control her own fate.

She held her breath as her left hand slowly went to her right. Then for the second time that day, she handed back an engagement ring. "I'm sorry, David. I've made a terrible mistake."

Chapter Fourteen

Monday morning, Sabrina entertained the idea of hiding out in the ladies' bathroom all day.

She examined her face in the mirror and thought she'd aged about ten years in the span of two days. After quickly splashing cold water on her cheeks, she blotted her face and assessed it again.

Yuck.

She was hopeless. There was no remedy for puffy, red eyes after a whole weekend of crying. Why was she even at work? To torture herself by seeing Jack again? She didn't know how she was going to handle working around him and loving him as she did. Seeing him on a daily basis would be a constant reminder of what she'd never have. What *they'd* never have together.

She needed to talk to someone before she broke down and made an even bigger fool of herself. Prying herself away from the mirror, she went in search of Chris.

Her friend was standing at the copier laughing with a cell phone in her hand, but one short look at Sabrina had her saying a hasty good-bye into it. "Oh my gosh," Chris said, raising a hand to Sabrina's forehead. "You look like death on a death watch."

Sabrina's shoulders slumped. "I'm okay." She shook her head. "No, I'm not okay."

Chris put down her phone and took hold of Sabrina's shoulders. "What's wrong?"

"I'm losing control of my life."

"Honey, nobody has complete control of their life. What fun would that be? Do you think I was in control when I got pregnant on my honeymoon?" Chris shook her head at herself. "I still don't know what happened there. But look how much fun I had, being newly married and pregnant with twins all at once." She made a face and rolled her eyes.

Sabrina couldn't help but grin. "Yeah, that was pretty amusing."

Chris shared her smile. "See? And I survived. Now tell Auntie Chris what could possibly be so terrible in your life."

"Okay, but you have to swear on your next pay raise that you won't breathe a word of this to anyone."

Chris made an exaggerated motion of crossing her heart. "It's in the vault."

Satisfied with that, Sabrina took a deep breath and rushed it all out at once. "Jack and I lied to Mr. Brenner and told him we were getting married, but Jack didn't really want to get married, and neither did I, and it made Mr. Brenner so happy. But now I *do* want to get married because I'm in love with him." She took another deep breath and waited.

Chris's calm expression turned to panic. "Wait, you're in

love with Mr. Brenner or Jack?"

"Jack."

"Whew, that's good." Her friend's expression relaxed. "*Soooo*...you're going to marry Jack, who you're in love with? What's the problem?"

"I'm not marrying Jack. Mr. Brenner just thinks that. At least for now."

"Why did you tell Mr. Brenner you were marrying Jack?"

Stalling, Sabrina raised her hand and pulled at her bottom lip. "So I could marry David," she said at last.

Chris blinked. "Honey, I'm going to slap you silly if you don't start making some sense."

Sabrina helplessly threw her hands in the air. "I know it doesn't make sense, but it's the truth. It's just complicated. But in a nutshell, I don't love David. I love Jack."

"How does Jack feel?" she asked.

Sabrina sadly shook her head.

Chris's face fell. "Oh. I'm sorry, honey. Are you sure?"

"I'm positive. He never really wanted me. It was always about the company and the national sales manager position."

"What are you going to do now?"

"I don't know." Sabrina sighed, covering her face with her hands. "But I'm freaking out here. I can't face Jack, and when Mr. Brenner learns the truth, I don't think I'll be able to face him, either. I should just quit."

"Whoa." Chris reached out and pulled Sabrina's hands away so she could look her in the eyes. "I know this is a difficult position for you, but don't do anything rash. Why don't you take some vacation time?"

"Vacation time?"

"Yeah, so you can think things through," Chris said soothingly. "You need a little separation from Jack. Clear your head."

"Maybe." She sniffed. It was starting to sound better and better the more she let it sink in. She knew it was running, but she didn't care. She'd run for as long as it took to have the pain go away.

Sabrina was gathering the last of her belongings when Jack suddenly appeared in front of her desk.

"Going somewhere?" he asked in way of greeting.

She paused, her fingers on her planner, then finally looked up, knowing when she did her heart would squeeze painfully.

And there it was. She placed her palm over the ache.

Jack's width blocked her view of the office area. She was left no choice but to give him her entire attention. He stood gazing down at her with those incredible eyes—such a perfect mixture of blue and gray that her insides fluttered. Would another man ever come close to having this kind of effect on her? "Um." She swallowed hard. "I decided to take some time off."

"This is sudden." His eyes began to roam her desk. "Going anywhere special?"

"Not sure yet."

"Is David going with you?"

She hesitated. "No."

His jaw seemed to relax with his stance. "Do you think it's safe to travel by yourself these days? Are you driving or flying? Because if you really wanted to, I could—"

"Jack, what's with the questions? When I told your dad, he didn't have a problem with me going someplace by myself at all. Don't worry," she added, "I didn't spill the beans about our fake engagement. I wouldn't want to ruin your promotion."

He stared at her with open disbelief. "That's not what I was talking about at all. It doesn't matter to me if you told my dad the truth or not. He's going to find out you're reengaged to David tomorrow night."

She slipped her hands under her desk so he wouldn't notice the absence of her ring. She didn't want to hear I-told-you-so right now. She didn't have the energy for it.

Jack reached out and touched her. Briefly, with his hand on her shoulder, but she still felt as though it were resting there. Or maybe she just wanted it to be there. "Look," he said. "I wanted to come here and tell you that despite how I acted the other day, I really am happy for you and David."

Jack couldn't have known, but that was the last thing on earth she needed to hear. "I thought you were against David?" she asked. "Against the marriage? Against marriage in general?"

He shrugged. "It doesn't seem to be in the cards for me, but hey, whatever makes you happy, right? I mean, it's not every day you find someone who has the ability to convert your insides to Jell-O with the smallest of smiles, or makes you do the damnedest things for her. *Him*," he corrected.

She stared at him, afraid that if she spoke she'd end up breaking apart into a million tiny pieces. Waves of nausea began to flood her stomach. How could she tell him she wasn't getting married? Especially after all she'd put him through.

Jack rounded her desk to take both of her hands in his and squeezed them gently. "I hope David knows how lucky he is to have you."

Lucky? Ha! David was lucky *not* to marry her. She didn't even know her own feelings. How could she have not seen earlier how much she was in love with Jack?

Jack dropped his arms. "I'll see you when you come back then."

She smiled. She wasn't sure it was much of one, but she supposed it was enough because he grinned back at her. Then, giving her a quick wink, he walked straight into his father's office.

I'll see you when you come back.

No, she thought as her eyes bordered with tears. She wouldn't be seeing him. Because right then and there, she decided she would not be coming back.

Chapter Fifteen

"Wait. You're *not* getting married?"

Jack numbly shook his head at his father and wished with every hair on his thick blockhead that he hadn't quit smoking. He could use a couple of World Fair cigars right about now. He figured if he couldn't be honest with Sabrina, he could at least be honest with his father. But the expression on his dad's face made it more difficult to explain than he'd expected.

Jack wasn't exactly doing cartwheels over the news himself. It tore at his insides thinking Sabrina was going to marry another man. Just when he finally found someone worth risking his feelings on, she refused to acknowledge what was happening between them. Every time he touched her, he swore he saw actual sparks. Sabrina had to have sensed it too, and if she'd felt just a fraction of what he felt for her, he wouldn't be sitting here in a restaurant breaking the sad truth to his dad.

He and Sabrina would be engaged for real.

Leonard Brenner looked at his son sympathetically. "What did you do?"

"I didn't *do* anything." Stalling, Jack brushed around some bread crumbs on the tablecloth. "We, uh, were never engaged in the first place." He spoke quietly, almost hoping his father's hearing wasn't as good as it used to be. "We lied."

"For God's sake, Jack, why would you do something like that? And why would Sabrina go along with it?"

Alarmed his father had the wrong impression of Sabrina, his eyes shot up. "It's not her fault," he said more intensely than he wanted. "She didn't want to lie to you. The woman's a saint—an absolute freaking saint. It was all my fault. I made her do it."

Without another word to Jack, his dad shot his arm out for the waiter and ordered a scotch. No ice. The waiter was already out of earshot, but his dad leaned in and lowered his voice anyway. "It's a good thing your mother's dead, because this would have done the job just as well. Have you lost your mind?"

"I know," Jack moaned, running his hands through his hair. "Sabrina wondered the same thing."

Squeezing his lids closed, his father rubbed methodically between his eyes. "I can't believe you would orchestrate this whole charade. I'm disappointed in you and Sabrina."

Jack sighed. "I didn't do this to hurt you. I thought it was what you wanted."

"Of course it's what I wanted!"

"Well, there you go."

"But for the right reasons! And I'd like it to be *true*." His father looked like he'd realized he had shouted and glanced around the dining room with some embarrassment.

"I'm sorry. I *am* sorry," Jack insisted when his father turned dubious eyes toward him. "But at least two out of three isn't bad."

"What do you mean, two out of three?"

"It's what *you* wanted; it's what *I* wanted. It's just not going to happen."

His dad's expression softened before him, centimeter by centimeter. "I don't understand."

"I'm completely in love with her." The words were coming easier and easier to him. Too bad they'd never be spoken to the one who really mattered. "That's the truth," he added.

"You are? So what's the problem? Did she turn you down?"

He shook his head. "I never got the chance to ask. She's back with her old fiancé."

His dad's brows wrinkled farther into a deep gray *V*. "Oh. I'm sorry, son. I never thought in a million years she wouldn't fall in love with you."

Jack's eyes narrowed. "What do you mean you never thought she wouldn't fall in love with me?"

His dad stilled then cleared his throat. "I guess I have some confessing to do too," he said sheepishly.

"Oh, no," he muttered.

"There were never any bad rumors about your reputation. Although I wasn't thrilled with your recent behavior, the board never mentioned anything to me. I made it all up. I was afraid you weren't balancing your life. Work had become an obsession to you. And well, I've always been fond of Sabrina… Naturally, I thought you two would be attracted to each other, so I might have thrown you together for more than work reasons."

Jack laughed mirthlessly at his father's attempt at match-making. The old man knew him well—maybe *too* well—and had picked a woman for him that he may not have noticed on his own otherwise. But they both didn't count on her not reciprocating the feeling.

"I guess my pain must seem infinitely smaller to what you're going through right now," his father said.

He had no idea.

Jack was getting pretty tired of that pain, too. Worrying he was becoming too vulnerable, he tried to bury it with cynicism. "Yeah well, I got what I deserved. Who could blame her? She knows me as a self-serving playboy. Not exactly a trait a woman comes running toward when she's looking for her soul mate."

"Stop beating yourself up. You're a good man. Someone I am very proud of and happy to see run this company one day."

Jack laughed again, despite the disgust he had toward the whole situation—and particularly himself. "I didn't do a very good job of showing her that."

"I saw how you've been with her," his dad countered. "That couldn't have been *all* for my benefit."

No. It wasn't. Somewhere in the middle of their pretending, it had turned very real. But she had her beliefs about fate and destiny and if that damn psychic of hers didn't see she and Jack together, it was a no-win situation.

"Maybe that's true, Dad, but Sabrina has certain preconceived notions of what she wants, and I couldn't compete with that. Or at least, she wouldn't let me compete."

When his father didn't comment further, Jack shook

his head at himself and looked away. And that's when his evening completely bottomed out.

Perfect, he thought, as David walked into the dining room. Just great. Speak of the so-called psychic's pet himself.

Jack had already figured out that Boston was a small enough city that he'd probably have to run into the happy couple sooner or later. But did it have to be this soon? The wide smile David paraded in with made Jack want to punch it clear through to the back of his skull. But Sabrina had made her choice and he was going to have to deal with it. Resigning himself to seeing Sabrina's equally happy expression, he waited for her to appear.

A redhead popped into view instead.

Jack's eyes narrowed. It was the same woman David had taken to the Ram's Horn. *What have we here?* Eyes glued to the couple, he couldn't miss how David took the woman's coat, then gave her a quick kiss on the cheek before turning away.

Jack almost bolted from his seat. David was cheating on Sabrina. On *his* Sabrina! The guy was a bigger jerk than Jack ever imagined—and his imagination ran pretty wild. That's it. There would be no saving the good doctor now.

"Excuse me, Dad," Jack said, standing up and shrugging out of his sports coat. He began rolling up his sleeves with his gaze aimed at David like a hunter not wanting to lose sight of his quarry. "I need to say hello to an old friend." *And perhaps rearrange some prominent features on his face.*

David sauntered to the coat check. He gave the coats to the girl and turned around with the ticket in his hand. That's when Jack came up behind him and shoved him into the men's bathroom.

"What the hell are you doing, Brenner?" David huffed, stumbling against a urinal. "I dropped my ticket."

"You're lucky I don't drop your face."

David paled. "What? What's the matter with you?"

"I want to know what's the matter with *you*. I saw the redhead you're with."

"Yes, she's something, isn't she?"

Jack lunged and grabbed the front of David's dress shirt, twisting it so his fists where just below his chin. "You shouldn't be with her," he growled.

David coughed as Jack leaned his knuckles against his throat. "If you...want to...date...her..."

"I'm not interested in dating her," he shot. "What do you think Sabrina would say about who you're with? You know Sabrina. Your *fiancée*."

David's face colored red, but he managed a hoarse response. "Sabrina's...not my...fiancée anymore."

Stunned, Jack quickly loosened his hold on David's shirt but didn't let go. *"What?"*

"She broke off our engagement."

"She did?"

David's countenance suddenly turned confident at Jack's obvious bewilderment. "Yes. Now get your damn paws off me, Brenner."

Jack let go and stepped back. David's hands went to his neck, and he warily watched Jack, as if he expected another attack. Normally that would have made Jack grin. Instead all he could think about was that Sabrina had broken off her engagement despite her reasoning for wanting David in the first place.

This changes everything. What happened between the

time he'd seen Sabrina and now? Jack wasn't sure what it meant, but maybe there was a chance for him yet. Maybe a little luck was on his side after all.

He took in David's rumpled appearance. The doctor would have some interesting explaining to do to his dinner date. "It's a shame about your shirt," he tossed out as he turned to the door. Jack could've sworn he heard David threaten something about calling the police if he ever touched him again, but Jack kept walking.

He was a man on a mission.

When he came back to the table, his father was in the process of eating his appetizer. "Dad, I have to go," he announced.

His father's head shot up, and he stopped chewing, swallowing so fast he almost choked. "What are you talking about? We just ordered our meal."

"Cancel mine. We'll have to do this another time."

"Another time? Now I know you've completely lost your mind. What's so important that you have to rush off right this second?"

Jack grabbed a dinner roll and grinned. "I have to go propose to my fiancée."

• • •

Maddie grabbed her hand and pulled her through the door of Madame Butterfly's Psychic Readings. "C'mon, Sabrina. This was your idea."

"I know, but I don't think I can take the journey-type stuff right now. Maybe after dinner." *Or a few stiff drinks.*

Maddie frowned at her. "Honey, you need closure.

Madame Butterfly said you and David would get back together and you did. Now let's go get her advice. It might
make you feel better."

Sabrina swiped at her eyes with the backs of her hands.
She couldn't handle any more "advice." She'd botched her
life enough. All she wanted to do now was forget. Forget
about her almost mistake with David. Forget about the lies.
And forget about Jack and the way she felt in his arms and
would never feel again.

Yeah. Good luck with all that.

Time away would help. Or so she hoped. Come Monday
morning, she'd tell Mr. Brenner she wasn't going to return to
work. He'd probably be grateful to get rid of her after her
dishonesty. She had no idea what she was going to do, but
with her experience she was reasonably sure she could find
another mutual-fund company.

But not another Jack.

It was just as well she wouldn't find another man like
him. She'd only have her heart battered and broken into
a thousand pieces all over again. Maybe she was meant to
be alone. Her journey. She'd end up one of those scary old
people children make fun of. It didn't sound so far-fetched
to her now.

Sabrina shook her head at her friend, her heart feeling
heavy and listless.

Maddie sighed. "Okay. Whatever you want. But this
would be good to get over… *Jack.*"

"Yeah, I want to get over Jack too."

Maddie pointed. "No. I mean, there's Jack."

Sabrina whirled around as Jack stepped through the
door of Madame Butterfly's. She blinked twice to be sure.

Oh my gosh, what is he doing here?

His white peacoat combined with dark jeans made for a dramatic combination as he stood before her. Once she caught her breath, she looked at his ruggedly handsome face and found her heart pumping out of control all over again. She wet her lips and fought to keep her voice even. "Jack, I—I thought you were having dinner with your dad tonight."

Jack shrugged, slipping his hands into his jacket pockets. "Something suddenly came up."

She studied him a moment, but his features were unreadable. He just stood there, those gray-blue eyes trained on hers and smelling of soap and that essence that was so pure Jack. It was enough to cause her head to float right up to the ceiling. "I'm getting a psychic reading," she said inanely.

He smiled, his dimples making him go from good-looking to star-studded handsome in less than thirty seconds. "I know. Mrs. Metzger told me you were here."

Sabrina held in a sigh. Of course Mrs. Metzger had told him she was here. Her landlady knew too much about her life, but not that Sabrina was trying to avoid seeing Jack at all costs.

Maddie cleared her throat behind them. "Uh, maybe I'll go and get my reading on that guy Carson I just met. This way you two can…catch up." She gave Sabrina a weak smile. "Good luck," she whispered, then slipped into the back room as fast as her heeled boots would let her.

Sabrina let out a nervous laugh. "You'll have to excuse Maddie. She forgot you and I saw each other at work this afternoon. There's not that much for us to catch up on."

"I'm not so sure. What do we have here?" Jack took a

few steps closer and lifted her right hand, making a show of inspecting it. "No ring?" he asked, his eyebrow quirking up. "Hmm…are you waiting for a full moon to put it on? Or did you see a black cat?"

She snatched her hand back. "Did you come here for some other reason than to offer up superstitious tips and annoy me?"

"Actually, I did. I came here looking for you, since we're friends and you consider yourself the all-around expert on love and marriage. Therefore you should be the first to know."

"Know what?"

"I met a woman recently." He paused and studied the ground, as if searching for the right words. "I'm going to ask her to, well, you know."

Blood began to pound in her head. A feeling of dread came fast and sharp up her spine. "What are you thinking of asking her?" *If your tie matches your eyes? What her zodiac sign is? Who she voted for in the last presidential election? What?!*

"You know, I'm going to ask her to…take the plunge with me."

Her heart stopped, and she blinked several times as if it could rewind that last statement. "Take the plunge?"

"Yeah. You know, tie the —"

She held up a hand. "*Yes,* I know."

Her heart started again and began to beat in a violent rhythm at the thought of Jack asking someone else to marry him. This was her worst nightmare—doubled. Breath coming in short pants, she turned away. She managed two short steps, then whirled around again. "You most certainly *cannot.*"

His eyebrows shot up. "I cannot?"

"No! You—you can't even say the actual words, for goodness's sake."

"Oh, that?" Jack shrugged. "I'm confident enough that when push comes to shove the words will come out nice and smooth." He gave her a toothy grin. "Like peanut butter."

More like chunky peanut butter. "You've got to be joking."

He drew himself up tall, his expression devoid of any teasing. "I'm totally serious."

"But why the change of heart? You told me you never wanted to get married."

He rubbed his chin. "I think it was you. What you did to get David back, what you went through for love. Must be pretty special. Special enough for me to realize I wanted it in my life too. Then there was all that talk you gave me about being afraid of my feelings. I guess it finally sunk in."

Her eyes widened. *Oh, no. This man doesn't sound like Jack at all.* He sounded like the kind of man she *hoped* Jack would sound like. He was saying the words *she* longed to hear. But they weren't aimed at her. They were going to belong to some other woman. What had she done?

She'd created a marriage-craving *monster.*

"You can't enter into a relationship like that lightly," she said, finally finding her voice and trying to rekindle any of the same anti-commitment feelings he once had. "You hardly know this woman."

"I've known her as long as I've known you. When you feel a certain way about someone you should let him or her know. No matter what. Don't you agree?"

"You're right," she blurted. She didn't mean to tell him the truth. But the words were gushing out before she could stop them. "This is all a big mistake. Jack, I'm no love expert, but I do know that I don't love David. I'm not wearing his ring because I gave it back. And now you want to get married because of everything I said. This is so terrible."

She threw herself into Jack's arms, unable to support herself any longer, and with better luck than she'd been having these past few months, he readily caught her.

"Whoa. Hey, now. Don't do this," he said with a hint of panic in his voice. "You're getting yourself worked up for nothing."

"Nothing?" she sobbed into his chest. "It's not nothing. I don't want you marrying someone else. I want you to marry *me*." She felt his fingers tighten on her arms, but she couldn't bring herself to look at him. "I know, I know. I can't believe it either. I feel so stupid. You're not at all what I wanted."

A strangled sound came from his throat, and then he cupped her cheeks with his hands and brought her face up. "Okay, okay, let's not ruin the moment any further. That's not exactly what a man wants to hear from the woman he's about to propose to."

His words vaulted through her brain and landed with swift precision in her heart. "Propose?"

Smiling, he wiped the tears from her cheeks with his thumbs. "Brie, I already knew that you and David broke up before I came over here. Your poker face is lousy, by the way."

"I always did tell you I was a terrible liar." Her lips trembled. "You knew? But why didn't you tell me?"

"I wasn't sure what your reasons were for breaking

ANCÉ ᗷy ᖴATE

off your engagement with David. I frankly don't give— I don't care. I just wanted to make sure you felt something— *anything*—for me."

"I do—"

The pads of his thumbs closed her lips. "Hold that thought. I've been trying to get this out for days now." Dropping his hands, he cleared his throat. "I want you to know that what I said before was true. You did make me see that the life you were after with David was worth it. It made me think that marriage was worth the risk. Only…the more I was around you, the more I only wanted to take that risk with *you*."

She opened her mouth, but he silenced her by giving her a look that told her if she interrupted again, he'd change his mind.

"Look, maybe I'm not who your psychic predicted and that all your signs might not point to me," he continued, "but I promise to always be by your side and to always make you happy. I want to be your family." His eyes never leaving hers, he took her hands in his.

They were strong and solid and warmed her from the outside to the center of her soul.

"I love you," he told her. "Please, marry me."

Not only did his words humble her, but the love and tenderness she saw in his eyes made her want to weep all over again. "Yes. I love—"

In one forward motion, she was in his arms, his mouth covering hers before she could even finish accepting his proposal. She clung to him, afraid if she didn't, she'd wake up and find this all a dream. She fit against him perfectly, as if she were made for him. As if they were one. As if he was her soul mate.

Jack broke the kiss and took hold of her face with hands that weren't completely steady. "Are you sure, Brie? I don't ever want you to have doubts. It's okay if you want to ask Madame Butterfly for advice while we're here."

She smiled and another tear mixed from love and happiness slid down her cheek. "No, Jack. I couldn't be more sure. I didn't fall in love with you because you were something I wanted you to be, or because of signs from above I thought I was getting. In fact, the only sign I need is right here," she said, taking his hand and placing it over her heart.

Jack brought his lips to hers, and she suddenly felt transported on some wonderful, wispy cloud. Her mind lost consciousness for several seconds, but when he finally pulled back, she managed to form coherent words. "I think that's a good sign too," she said with a sigh.

"Think?" He chuckled, leaning his forehead against hers. "Sweetheart, I better make you a one hundred percent believer."

She laughed as he kissed her again. His mouth was hot, but still sweet, and because she knew him so well—very determined. But Jack didn't need to convince her. There was no thinking about it. At last, she knew she had found her true love. Her family. No comparisons needed, no superstitions or doubts. Only the love they felt for each other and the future they would now have together.

She had a feeling her parents were smiling.

Epilogue

Six months later

The summer sun's rays shone through the window of the Tradewind Hotel, casting an orangey glow onto the empty dance floor. Jack would have much preferred the Four Seasons, but Sabrina wanted to hold their reception at the place she said she first started to fall in love with him: where she found out he secretly liked *Mamma Mia*.

How could he say no?

Heart full, Jack stood by his wife and kissed her hand before the band announced their arrival. Sabrina's gaze met his and a smile curved across her lips.

Jack might have rushed their wedding plans a bit, but if it were up to him, they would have eloped. Sabrina fought him on that. Six months was the compromise, and not surprisingly to him, she managed to pull it off without a glitch.

"Ladies and gentlemen, please stand and join me in

welcoming the new Mr. Jack and Mrs. Sabrina Brenner."

He squeezed her hand. "That's our cue."

Applause broke out as they walked onto the dance floor, and as soon as the band began to play "Our Love is Here to Stay," he swept her into his arms. Sabrina looked up at him with eyes that glowed a deep ocean blue. Eyes he looked forwarding to gazing into every day for the rest of his life.

She sighed. "How lucky are we?"

"If you play your cards right, you'll get even luckier tonight." He leaned down and nuzzled her neck, eliciting a giggle from her throat.

She looked over his shoulder and then her smile lost some of its light. "Jack, I'm a little worried about Maddie."

"Maddie?" he asked, glancing in her direction.

Maddie stood alone by the bar, toying with the flowers in her bouquet, her shoulders slumped. But as soon as she noticed he and Sabrina watching her, she pasted on a giant grin and waved at them. Yeah, something was definitely up with her.

"She hasn't been able to find a job or a man in months. She didn't even bring a date to our wedding."

Jack sighed, knowing if he didn't act fast, Sabrina would worry about her friend all night. "Tell you what, as soon as we get back from our honeymoon, I'll see if I can set her up with a broker I know."

Her face lit up. "You are the best husband ever." She kissed his cheek. "Do you happen to know anyone with a lot of hair?"

"I'm hoping there's a sensible explanation that's going to follow that."

"Well, Madame Butterfly said—"

"Oh, no," he chided, waving a mocking finger at her. "No, no, *no*. We're not going there. Not tonight. Not ever."

"You're absolutely right. That psychic stuff doesn't matter anymore." Then she touched her lips to his, a soft kiss that whispered the true words in her heart. He could never get enough of her mouth and wanted more, but they had an audience watching.

"All right then," he said with a nod. "You had me worried there for a minute."

"Well, then, let me officially put your worries to rest right now. Jack Brenner, I love you and nothing is ever going to change that."

"Not even when I start making demands on you as your boss? As you probably are aware, I can be hell to work—"

She quieted him with another kiss, and when she drew back, she was grinning. "I wouldn't push your luck," she whispered in his ear.

Jack didn't dare.

Acknowledgments

Kisses and thanks to the best critique partners EVAH over at Passionate Critters group.

Thanks again to my mom, who is an astrology buff and psychic believer. I may not agree with your beliefs but they did provide me with excellent book fodder.

Thank you to fellow Bliss author Susan Meier and her awesome online class CAN THIS MANUSCRIPT BE SAVED? The answer I learned was YES. Yes, this manuscript can. Check out her class!

Super special thanks to my editors Stacy Abrams and Alycia Tornetta. You guys always provide such great feedback and have excellent eyes. I'm really blushing at how many times you had to highlight "just" and "all."

And lastly, to everyone over at Entangled Publishing: The camaraderie and support is still going strong.

About the Author

Jennifer Shirk has a bachelor's degree in pharmacy — which has in *no way* at all helped her with her writing career. But she likes to point it out, since it shows that romantic-at-hearts come in all shapes, sizes, and *mind-numbing* educations.

She writes sweet (and sometimes even funny) romances for Samhain Publishing, Montlake Romance, and Entangled Publishing. Recently, her novel *Sunny Days for Sam* won the 2013 Golden Quill Published Authors Contest for Best Traditional Romance.

Lately she's been on a serious exercise kick. But don't hold that against her.

http://www.jennifershirk.com/

https://twitter.com/JenniferShirk

Also, if you liked this book, sign up for Jennifer's newsletter be the first to hear about my next release and a chance to win some awesome prizes.

15688805R00135

Made in the USA
Middletown, DE
17 November 2014